"I'm Tonia Konig," she said finally, crossing her arms and leaning against the fireplace.

"I know," I informed her. "I've seen you interviewed on television. I even started to read your book *A World Without Violence.*"

That clearly surprised her. She blinked several times, perhaps elevating me from the ranks of the functionally illiterate.

"Started?" she asked suspiciously.

"Mmhmm. But I couldn't figure out how to apply the theory. It seemed kind of irrelevant to my line of work."

She actually snorted, and looked over at Valerie, who had collapsed on the couch. Valerie shrugged helplessly.

I held up my hands. "I think I can summarize our differences."

Tonia exhaled sharply. Valerie nodded.

I continued, "Tonia would prefer to have Henry Kissinger or maybe Jesse Jackson do the job, seeing as how Gandhi is dead. Valerie, on the other hand, doesn't give a damn who does it as long as it gets done efficiently and discreetly."

"Don't you dare patronize me, you little thug," Tonia said in a sub-zero voice.

"Oh God," Valerie muttered, raking her hair.

"I'm not patronizing you," I told Tonia. "Believe me, I have nothing but respect for your work. But I have to tell you that none of your theories, nothing you believe in, is going to do you a damned bit of good with this."

The Always Anonymous Beast

Lauren Wright Douglas

NAIAD

1987

Printed in the United States of America
First Edition

Cover design by The Women's Graphic Center
Edited by Katherine V. Forrest
Typesetting by Sandi Stancil

Library of Congress Cataloging-in-Publication Data

Douglas, Lauren Wright, 1947—
    The always anonymous beast.

    I. Title
PS3554.08263A79 1987   813′.54   87-20342
ISBN 0-941483-04-5

ABOUT THE AUTHOR

Lauren Wright Douglas was born in Canada in 1947. She grew up in a military family and spent part of her childhood in Europe. As a child she enjoyed telling stories to friends, and began to write poetry and fiction at age nine. After graduating from college in Canada, she taught high school English and Physical Education, was a French translator, a newspaper editor, and a financial advisor. She has published magazine and newspaper articles, essays, poetry, screenplays, and short stories. Lauren moved to the U.S. Southwest in 1983 and is now a full-time writer. *The Always Anonymous Beast* is her first published novel.

DEDICATION

For Margaret Molloy, who taught me the difference between a simile and a metaphor; Pansy Jean and Robert Douglas, who never discouraged my interest in books; Jeanne, who always believed in me; Gloria and Velda, who did on-site research; Joan, who put up with all the histrionics; and Martha, who read, criticized, and reread.

Jealousy cannot forget for all her sakes . . .
Her holy unholy hours with the always anonymous beast.

Dylan Thomas

MONDAY

Chapter 1

"I'm being blackmailed," she told me. Direct, right to the point, just as in her television interviews.

We stood together at the seawall at Victoria's inner harbor on a gusty afternoon in April. The sky was pearl grey, the sea pewter, and only a thin smear of lemon light on the horizon indicated that the sun had not forgotten us entirely. Spring in the Pacific Northwest is an iffy season.

I decided to let her talk. Oh, I knew who she was all right—I recognized her as soon as she got out of her car and came walking toward me. Even with her attempt at a disguise—oversized dark glasses, beige raincoat buttoned up to her throat—hers was not a face you would forget. Along with half the population of Victoria, I saw it every night, anchoring

3

the six o'clock news. To my credit, I didn't say, "Gee, aren't you . . . ?" Instead, I waited.

She took off her dark glasses and turned to face me. Her eyes were moss green and troubled. I tried a reassuring smile. No response. Maybe she needed prompting after all.

"So, tell me about it," I urged.

"Dammit, I'm trying," she said in obvious distress. She gave me a look that I knew well, albeit vicariously. It was a look reserved for corrupt union leaders, double-talking politicians, and child molesters. I cringed just a little.

"How do I know you can help?" she asked me.

"How do you know I can't? You haven't told me a thing."

"What I mean is . . ." She chewed her lip.

"What you mean is, you've never heard of me, you haven't the faintest idea about what I really do or if I'm any good at it, and besides, where's my luxuriously appointed office?"

It worked. She smiled. Just a little.

"Who recommended me to you?"

"My attorney. Virginia Silver."

"Well, do you trust her?"

"Oh, yes. Unqualifiedly."

"Well, that's a start, anyway." I sighed. "As for the rest, what I do is simple. I try to help people. People who get caught in messes and don't know how to get out. People who the system can't help." Seeing the skepticism on her face, I added, "And I don't do it for nothing. I'm no Good Samaritan."

She nodded a little, as if this made sense. Economics usually does. "What *is* your fee?" she wanted to know.

"I charge two hundred and fifty dollars a day plus expenses. I need a thousand up front. When I'm finished you'll get a report and a statement from me detailing how I spent your money."

She thought this over. "All right."

"Now, as for whether I'm any good at what I do, you should ask Virginia. And I don't have an office. I work at home. For obvious reasons I prefer not to meet clients there. So we meet somewhere else."

She nodded again.

"So, why don't you briefly tell me what you need me to do, and I'll briefly tell you if I think I can do it."

She smiled again, a trifle weakly, then let out the breath she had been holding. "As I said, someone is blackmailing me. Well, trying to."

"Trying to?"

"I haven't paid any money yet."

"Good. Go on."

"He said he'd call Monday night."

Monday night—tonight? She did believe in living dangerously. "What time and where?"

"Eight o'clock. I'll give you the address."

"So what does this guy have on you?"

She looked angry. "Letters."

"Written by you?"

"Yes."

"To whom?"

She actually flinched. "To another woman."

"Has she heard from the blackmailers? Your lover?"

She flinched again, and I suddenly realized that she was bitterly ashamed of her involvement with this other woman. I felt sorry for her—that, of course, was part of the blackmailer's hold over her. "Yes, we've both heard from him. Despite the fact that we have unlisted numbers. We both got the same note, telling us what he had. Then a phone call saying he'd call tonight."

I sighed. "This may sound silly, but have you considered going to the police?"

She skewered me with that accusing look. "Yes, it sounds silly."

5

"All right. And you're very sure you can't afford the publicity? Scandals die down pretty fast. Even scandals like this. In a week no one will even remember who you had an affair with, let alone care."

There was that look again.

"Okay, okay," I capitulated. "So what do you want me to do?"

"Get the letters back. Make him leave me—us, alone." She shrugged. "If you can't, we'll have to pay, I suppose."

"No," I told her.

"No?"

"Don't even think about paying. Blackmailers are bloodsuckers. He'll drain you. And not only of money. There are other things to lose, too."

She shuddered. "Well, can you help?" She chewed her lip again, a nervous gesture no one ever saw on the air.

"It *is* the sort of thing I do," I said cautiously. "I have helped people in similar situations. But we'd have to get a few things straight." I tried to look authoritative. "You'd have to do what I tell you."

She nodded.

"And I have to meet your lover. I need to talk to both of you."

She closed her eyes for a moment. "All right," she said, a little tentatively. I could tell this was not a threesome she was anticipating.

"And last, if we blow it, if I try and fail, then you have to give me your word that you'll consider — just consider — disclosure of whatever is in the letters. Your disclosure. Your initiative. Go public. Put it in the papers. Call a press conference. Rent a skywriting plane. In short, beat the blackmailer to it."

She didn't hesitate. "All right, I'll consider it. And if those are all your terms, I agree to them."

I shrugged. "Okay. Write me a check and let's get started. Oh, better give me your address, too."

She fished a leather-bound checkbook and a gold Cross pen out of her purse. "To whom do I make this payable?" she asked.

"To me. Caitlin Reece."

"I'm Val Frazier," she said, handing me my advance, and a slip of paper with her address written on it.

"I know," I told her, putting the check in my windbreaker pocket. I held out my hand. A little hesitantly, she took it. We shook.

She raised an eyebrow. "That's it?" she asked. "No contract? Don't I have to sign *something*?"

I smiled. "This isn't the movies. I told you the terms of my employment. You agreed. I took your money. Now I'm working for you."

That seemed to cheer her a little. "Thank God someone is," she said. She put on her dark glasses and turned up the collar of her raincoat. "Now what?"

"I'll come over just before eight. We'll take it from there."

As she was leaving, I asked the question. "Why me? There are plenty of people who do this kind of thing. Some are even quite good at it."

She turned back to look at me, inscrutable behind the dark glasses. "Part of it was Virginia's recommendation. I was told you're one of those who are very good at it."

"And the other part?"

"You're . . . you're . . ."

Comprehension dawned. I decided to help her out. We might have stood there all afternoon while she choked on the word. "I'm a lesbian," I said. "Is that it?"

"Yes," she replied faintly, then turned and fled to the sanctuary of her car.

Chapter 2

After I watched Val's white Porsche wheel out of the parking lot, I zipped my windbreaker a little higher and turned back to study the sea. Usually it inspired me—I love it in all its moods—but after my talk with Val I felt irritable and depressed. Her inability to accept the fact that she loved (or had loved) another woman boded ill not only for this case but for Val personally. I tried my best to direct my speculation to the job ahead of me, but found myself wondering how Val had ever gotten involved with another woman, given her inability to even say the world lesbian. Would her lover be equally ill at ease? I supposed that in Val's job a certain amount of circumspection and discretion was necessary, but surely one's private life was one's own.

I recalled my own years of obfuscating the truth—the years I spent in law school and in the Crown Prosecutor's office—and felt a twinge of sympathy. I'd had precious little time to pursue romance, but still, the necessary lies were extremely tedious. I recalled being irked at the need to deceive my classmates or colleagues about who my dates *really* were, but I was never ashamed of the fact that I loved women. And I certainly never felt guilty. Now thank heavens, life was infinitely easier. I had to answer to no one.

But Val? I shrugged. Her personal life, like mine, was her own business. She was entitled to make as huge a mess of it as she wanted. I had been hired to retrieve the letters. Nothing more. But still, Val's attitude and the case were inextricably intertwined. Val's guilt not only gave the blackmailer a handle on her professional life, but it gave him power over her personal life as well. I sighed. Even if I got the letters back, thereby assuring Val that no one at the television station would ever know The Horrible Truth, the blackmailer would still have an edge. He would still know what she perceived to be a shameful secret. If he were thwarted in his financial demands, he might well, out of pure cussedness, phone any of her friends and plant this germ of suspicion. Did Val want to live with that threat hanging over her head? I couldn't have borne it. And what did she intend to do after the case was over? Scuttle back into her closet and nail the door shut?

A sudden urge to *do something* came over me. I looked at my watch. Not even four o'clock. Plenty of time.

* * * * *

It took me a few laps of the health club's pool to work up a good rhythm. Then I released my mind, to go where it would. After a few moments of aimless wandering, it returned, stubborn as a badger, to root out the question I had asked myself earlier: what made me think I could help Val. Or, more precisely: what made *me* think I could help Val.

As little as three years ago, I wouldn't have been able to. I would have been as baffled and frustrated as Val. As most people. But that was before Marc Bergeron, Jan Principal, and Texada Island.

* * * * *

At thirty-five, I had been a wreck. Washed-up, burned-out, and ready to pack it in. Seven years of working in the criminal justice system had just about finished me. Had I stayed, the Crown Prosecutor's office would surely have been my grave. I had seen one too many leering rapists, grinning child molesters, and smirking muggers elude justice. Marc Bergeron was the straw that broke this camel's back, and almost drove me over the line into madness. To understand that, however, you'd have to know a little bit about my mother's family.

The Llewelyns are a spooky bunch. My mother's two older sisters were as nutty as pecan groves. I remember my Aunt Fiona in particular. She was in her mid-fifties when madness overcame her, and the most appalling feature of it was the way it changed her physically. The summer I was twelve was the last time I ever saw her. She had changed from being a tall, stately, well-groomed, handsome woman to a stooped, wild-haired witch. A hag. God, only a few centuries ago she would have been burned at the stake. But the neighbors in the little town where my mother's family lived all accepted the fact that half of the Llewelyn womenfolk were destined to be wacko. Never the menfolk—which as a twelve-year-old I thought vastly unfair. Still do. Only the women. Dat ole X chromosome.

One evening as we all sat at dinner, Aunt Fee pouring coffee over her potatoes and humming something in a minor key, she looked across the table at me and declared in her harpy voice: "You've got it, too."

My brother snickered, and I surreptitiously kicked him.

"Got what, Aunt Fee?" I was a polite child, so I asked the question. But my heart had already descended into my Keds. I knew perfectly well what she was talking about.

She ignored me, and looked at my sniggering brother. "You don't," she said summarily. "Your sort never does. Your heads are too thick." And that was the end of the discussion. Until later that night.

Unable to sleep, I had crept downstairs for a glass of cold milk. And had run smack into Aunt Fiona sitting on a straight-backed chair in front of the open cellar door.

"Aunt Fee," I said, as soon as my heart stopped beating double time. "What are you doing here?" I knew my Uncle Daffyd had a hard time keeping track of my aunt, and I wondered if I should try to usher her upstairs to bed.

"Waiting," she told me.

"For what?"

She turned to look at me, and the expression on her face made my heart turn over. She wasn't crazy at all, at least not for those few moments. She smiled. "Caitlin," she said, evidently pleased to see me.

"Yes, Aunt Fee. But what are you waiting for?" I wanted to know.

She looked at me as if I, not she, were the crazy person here. "Why, for the Dark Lady, of course." She pointed to the Stygian depths of the cellar. "She'll come, sooner or later. And I'll be here." She clasped her hands over her breast and began to rock a little.

Scared to death, I asked the question. "What does she want, Aunt Fee?"

But my aunt had slid back down into madness again, and was unable — or unwilling — to answer. Finally I left her there, after first making sure that all the doors were locked.

12

The following winter Aunt Fiona died. And the specter of the Dark Lady began to haunt me. I began to have nightmares in which a tall figure clad in black burst out of some gloomy cave in search of me. And although I ran, I knew she would get me sooner or later. Just like she'd gotten Aunt Fee.

Well, she didn't, of course. And gradually the obsession left me. I stopped dreaming about dark ladies in the basement and got on with my life. But I wondered from time to time—was there something horrible lurking in my brain, ticking away like a time bomb? And why did it drive its possessors mad, turning them into gibbering idiots? It was all too melodramatic for me.

"It," of course, was a kind of rudimentary clairvoyance. And I finally just stopped worrying. There was nothing else to do. If I had it, I'd have to think of it as a sense, like vision, or touch. It certainly couldn't be gotten rid of. Maybe it could even be useful, I told myself. If it appears, just accept it—don't let it turn your brain to jelly as it had Fiona's.

So I made an accommodation with it. And a vow. It wasn't going to get me. I was going to be a lawyer, damn it, not a gypsy fortune teller. I told no one about my family's ability to "know" things before they had happened. Who wants to be thought weirder than they are?

It was another twenty-three years before I found that I had "it." And, as I said, I have Marc Bergeron to thank for the revelation.

You may remember the Bergeron case. The media had a field day with it. It started with the disappearance of little Annie Graves. It was her birthday. Her sixth birthday. Her dad had let her ride her newly painted bike to the local Seven-Eleven for a popsicle. A massive search operation was begun, but to no avail. It was as if the little girl had vanished into thin air. Four days later a Parksville cop stopped a man for speeding, and noticed that the left front fender of the car was slightly scratched and bore a smear of pink Dayglo paint. Annie's bike had been pink. The cop quite properly detained the man and called for assistance. Marc Bergeron was taken to Parksville police headquarters and questioned. He denied any knowledge of how the pink paint had gotten on his car. When an arrest (but no conviction) for child molestation was found on his record, he was taken into custody.

Fortunately, Annie's dad still had the spray paint can he had used. The paint on Bergeron's car matched the paint in the can. Officers were sent to Bergeron's house, but found nothing.

It was then the afternoon of the fourth day since Annie's disappearance. Bergeron's camper and boat, parked in his yard, had been searched, neighbors, friends, and co-workers questioned. Bergeron's locker at the garage where he worked as a mechanic had been opened, as had the trunks of the cars awaiting repair. Nothing. Time and tempers were growing short.

And through it all Bergeron smirked. With his previous arrest inadmissible in court, I could see him slipping away from us as the hours ticked away and we were unable to locate Annie, the bicycle, or anything else to conclusively tie the two of them together. We did not have a case. Of course, everyone hoped Annie would be found alive; however, in our hearts we knew she was dead. But what had he done with her? And where was the damned bicycle?

The CP gave Bergeron to me. And from the very first minute I saw him, I knew we had lost. Remember the scene at the end of *Psycho* when Anthony Perkins, as Mother, is sitting all alone in a chair in an otherwise empty room? His head is bent, and at the last minute he raises it and looks directly at the camera, and the demon looks at us out of his eyes. There is nothing human about him. Marc Bergeron looked at me the same way. And I knew it was all over. The criminal justice system wouldn't lay a glove on him. Even if we found the body, he would never stand trial. His attorneys would claim insanity.

14

My "knowing" — the Llewelyn prescience — was born the day I interviewed Bergeron for the first time.

As I sat opposite him, the information just popped into my consciousness: *Bergeron had another car*. I felt as though a low-voltage charge had just sizzled through my brain. Without even thinking about how I would explain this to the CP, I ran from the interview room to a phone. With the help of the British Columbia Insurance Corporation, which maintains up-to-date records on all vehicles, we traced the car that afternoon. It was parked at Bergeron's absent buddy's dilapidated farmhouse in Saanich, the windows taped up with newspapers, as if he were preparing to paint it. Inside was the sexually violated body of Annie Graves. She had suffocated. Her bicycle was in the trunk.

Marc Bergeron was declared unfit to stand trial by reason of insanity, and incarcerated in a psychiatric hospital outside Prince George. But not before I had spent enough time with him to know that he was no more insane than you or I. Neither crazy nor unintelligent, he was, instead, the most cold-blooded schemer I have ever encountered. He knew right from wrong—that was obvious because he had taken such pains to conceal Annie's body. Aside from the child molestation on his record, I suspected a score that had never seen the legal light of day. He had hinted at them under questioning, smirking all the while. Insane? No. Marc Bergeron had *chosen* to do these terrible things. But why?

That was the question I wanted answered, and it was the one answer that Bergeron withheld from me. Until the day he was scheduled to leave for Prince George. Prison authorities delivered a scrawled message to me from him, written in haste as he was leaving. Nothing incriminating—after all, he was insane, wasn't he? It was just one line on a piece of paper. *Because I can*, it read. Nothing more.

I resigned from the CP's office that afternoon. The criminal justice system had left Marc Bergeron untouched.

But it had chewed me up and spit me out. I no longer wanted to be a part of a mechanism that declared itself helpless in the face of the evil represented by the Marc Bergerons of the world. And I was convinced it *was* evil. Funny, I had never thought much about the concept before that time. And I hadn't thought for years about the Llewelyn clairvoyance. When confronted with both of them, I ran.

I rented a shack on Texada, in the Gulf Islands. On a cove that didn't have a name. And fished. Without a hook. Every day I motored out to an unnamed hunk of rock, dropped anchor, propped my pole against the side of the boat, and lay there and watched the clouds. Or the rain. At night, I drank myself to sleep. I lost twenty-five pounds, and all interest in life. If it hadn't been for Jan Principal, I might have gone down for the count.

One day in early April, Jan just appeared on the wharf as I was getting ready to go out to my hunk of rock. Tall, blond, disgustingly healthy, she looked me over critically, frowned, and said: "You look like hell."

"What's it to you?" I asked her, surprised at how difficult speech was. My voice was raspy, and my mouth had difficulty shaping the sounds. With a start, I realized I hadn't spoken to anyone in weeks.

She ignored the question, and came to stand between me and my boat, hands jammed in her parka pockets. "I bet you haven't had a bath since you got here."

"You lose," I told her. "I've been rained on three times. Now get out of my way."

She scowled, and drew herself up to her full six feet. "Rude, aren't you?" she said.

I lost my temper then. "Who the hell are you?" I shouted. "My mother? Leave me alone, dammit!"

"Listen, kid, you've been alone for two months," she said quietly. "Your rock is directly in line with my study window. I can't help but see you. Every time I look up from the

16

typewriter, there you are. Getting dirtier and skinnier." She looked me up and down. "You're pitiful. Whatever your problem is, surely it's not worth killing yourself over."

"I don't have a problem anymore," I told her. "I left it in the Crown Prosecutor's office. Now I'm free. And if you don't get off the end of my wharf, I'll heave you into the Pacific."

"I doubt that," she said.

My patience snapped. I tackled her, and we both hurtled off the end of the dock into the green water of the bay. It was much deeper than I had figured, and heart-stoppingly cold. I came up sputtering and gasping, treading water, but Jan was nowhere in sight. "Oh, shit!" I yelled, and went down for her.

Never believe the old myth that says drowning people come up three times. I submerged, and in the jade-colored murk at the bottom found Jan, struggling feebly, her waterlogged clothes weighing her down. I swam around behind her, grabbed a handful of her hair, and pushed myself off the bottom. Our heads broke the surface, and she began to choke and cough—a good sign. If she was breathing, she would be all right. But first I had to get her to shore. I towed her into shallow water, and when my heels brushed bottom, I let her go. She lurched out of the water and up the beach, where she collapsed on a driftwood log, coughing her guts out. As for me, the unaccustomed exertion had taken its toll. I managed to walk three steps toward the beach before I passed out, and as I fell back into the water I recall thinking with black glee that it would now finally all be over. Finis. The end.

I woke up in an unfamiliar bed, in someone else's pajamas, in a cozy room with a fire snapping in the hearth. I closed my eyes quickly. If this was a dream, it was sure a good one. I felt warm and safe. But where was I? My brain soon supplied a possibility—the blonde woman's cabin, across the bay. I cringed. If I had been she, I might have left my would-be murderer floating in the water like a dead carp. Instead, she must have dragged me out and transported me back to her place. I wondered how. I also wondered why I didn't remember any of it. A sick fatigue came over me then, and I closed my eyes and sank back into sleep.

When I awakened again, bright sunlight was flooding into the room. Jan was sitting in a chair by the window, reading. "You should have told me you couldn't swim," I managed.

She closed the book and looked over at me, raising one pale eyebrow. "What, and missed all that fun? Do I dare approach you, or will you tackle me again? Incidentally, I'm Jan Principal."

"Caitlin Reece," I said. "And you're safe. I don't feel up to tackling. But you'd better not get too close. As you remarked, I've neglected my personal grooming lately."

She laughed. "Well, as soon as you're able, you can visit the bathroom. It's just out the door to the left. And I've made chicken soup if you want some."

It was my turn to raise an eyebrow. "Why?" I wanted to know.

"Oh, let's just say that you were cluttering up my seascape," she said, smiling inscrutably. "Also, Virginia Silver is a friend of mine, too."

So Virginia had asked her to keep an eye on me. Somehow, I didn't mind too much. I had a shower, washed my hair, cut it, then washed it again before I was satisfied that I was clean. A fresh pair of pajamas had appeared in the bathroom while I was in the shower, and I put them on gratefully. My ablutions had taken the little strength I had, and I was happy to crawl back into bed. Chicken soup and crackers were waiting for me on the night table. I devoured every bit of the food—nothing had ever tasted so good. Then, rudely, I fell asleep again.

Three days later, I was able to get up and take a half-hearted interest in life. However, I still could not bear to watch television news or read the papers. I still wasn't up to coping with the real world. Jan supplied me with a steady stream of science fiction and fantasy novels, and we watched nature programs carried by PBS. She made it easy to play hooky. It wasn't until I had been there for three weeks that I realized what was happening to me—I was becoming more and more attracted to this wry, generous woman. I felt like a traitor—she had plucked me from a downhill slide to oblivion, offered me the hospitality of her house, and this was how I repaid her? But I could no more have stopped feeling the way I did than I could have stopped breathing.

The night I marched into her bedroom and made my confession, I felt as if I were going before a firing squad.

"The only thing I can think about these days is getting in bed with you, dammit," I said belligerently from the safety of the bedroom doorway. Then I waited.

She took off her reading glasses, put down the manuscript she had been revising, and looked at me. "Is the prospect that frightening?"

I swallowed nervously. "Yes, it is."

"It needn't be," she said.

"That's easy for you to say," I quipped, "but I'm not exactly an old hand at this sort of thing. In fact, um, well, I'm a little out of practice." That was some understatement. For the past seven years in the CP's office, and four years in law school before that, I had devoted my life mostly to work. And with a few exceptions, my romantic liaisons lately had been limited to the pages of novels.

To my infinite relief, she smiled. "This isn't something you forget how to do. Believe me."

"That's reassuring. Why do I feel so nervous, then?"

"I don't know. Come on over here and we'll discuss it."

I walked around the bed, weak-kneed, and sat beside her. "I feel like a fool," I confessed. "Maybe this isn't such a good idea."

She put her hands on my shoulders. "I think it's an excellent idea," she said, smiling. "You'll see—it's like riding a bicycle. It all comes back to you surprisingly quickly."

She was right—it did.

I stayed with Jan for three more weeks, until she had to go to Toronto on business. We both knew by then that what had happened between us could not be sustained. Our prickly personalities were too similar—we would have quickly come to the point where we couldn't stand to be with each other. But I saw our relationship end with plenty of anguished regret, and my time with her was one of the periods of my life I will always treasure. The day after she left, I took the ferry back to Victoria and rejoined the human race.

Jan Principal turned my life around in more ways than one. She gave me the time to heal myself, and to get to know myself. There was more to Caitlin Reece than a brain, she showed me—there were feelings, too. During the time I spent with Jan I decided what I was going to do. I had failed Annie Graves and her parents, but there were plenty of other people I could help. Even it if meant operating outside the law. Why? Because, to paraphrase Marc Bergeron, *I* could.

* * * * *

After fifty laps of the health club's pool, fifteen minutes in the sauna, and five minutes under the shower, I felt like going home and crawling into bed with a cat and a good book. Instead, I dried my hair and decided to go and fortify myself with a late lunch. Or an early dinner. As I dressed, I looked at myself critically in the mirror. Caitlin Reece, soon to be thirty-nine, five-foot-eight, 140 pounds. Not exactly a sylph. But a girlhood of running, jumping, riding, and swimming had resulted in muscles—muscles that had to be kept toned in sedentary middle age. I made a face at myself. Middle age. It sounded like a particularly dismal village in the British Isles.

20

And here we have Middle Age, just down the road from Girlhood-under-Bridge. And not quite as far as Greater Senility. I grimaced, examining my teeth. Still all mine, even if they weren't pearly white. I batted my eyes. Not too bad. Somewhere between green and grey. My complexion was okay—no warts or wens or wattles. And my hair was still reddish brown. Or brownish red. Not grey yet. All in all, I'd give myself a six and a half on the proverbial scale of ten. Well, maybe a seven. No prize, but nothing to be ashamed of, either.

* * * * *

A light rain had begun while I had been inside the restaurant stuffing myself, and I walked to my car feeling irritable and gloomy. By April, we west coast denizens have seen about as much rain as we can take. Fungus has begun to grow between our toes. Those who can afford it, flee south to dry out briefly in some infernal sun-blasted clime. Those of us who can't, remain bravely behind, growing more sodden and surly by the week.

Sneezing, I let myself into my MG, cursed the ill-fitting cloth convertible top, and started the wipers. I felt as though I were getting a cold, and shivered a little, wanting to go home. Instead, I forced myself to think about the business still ahead of me this evening. And Val. I switched on the heater, remembering Jan again and feeling lucky. Poor Val with her insupportable burden of shame and guilt. Well, that was her problem. Mine was getting the letters back. Nothing more.

Chapter 3

I made a quick trip home to pick up some things I figured I'd need. My living quarters are one-half of an old duplex on Monterey Street, solidly inside the village of Oak Bay. Oak Bay is, of course, part of Victoria—Canada's "best bloomin' city," or as the tour guides say "a little bit of Olde England transported to Canada." There's something special about cities by the sea—people seem happier there. It's as if the sea provides a permanence our lives lack—it was there yesterday; it will be there tomorrow. Despite its moods, you can count on it.

My house felt cold to me, and I turned up the thermostat a little. There was no furry grey body in his usual spot by the hot air register, so I figured Repo must be upstairs in my tenant's greenhouse, lolling under the growlight and keeping an eye on the sprouting catnip plants. What a life. Remind me to check the box labelled cat when the reincarnation requests are handed around. I filled his food dish with Meow Mix, and changed his water, just in case he deigned to put in a appearance for dinner.

My tenants, Malcolm and his wife Yvonne, displaced Australians, run a health food store in Oak Bay. It's a thriving business, and despite their own glowing good health, I resist being converted. Hearing about the alleged benefits of spirulina and evening primrose oil produces the same effect in me as do the intricacies of bubble memory, or selling stock short—my eyes glaze over, and five minutes after having been enlightened, I've forgotten every word.

From a locked cupboard in my study I took a tape recorder, telephone attachment, earphone, and, after a moment's deliberation, my Smith and Wesson .357 Magnum. Feeling a little chilly, I changed clothes quickly, into a pair of tan corduroy slacks and a white wool turtleneck. I clipped the gun to the back of my slacks and put on a tweed jacket that hung nicely, concealing the bulge. I do not have a license to carry a concealed weapon—they are almost impossible to obtain in Canada. So I try to forget that I'm breaking the law. As the wags say, better to be judged by twelve than carried by six. I also have a Colt .45 automatic, but I prefer the reliability of a revolver. There's nothing to jam. Critics might say that the .357 semi-wadcutter load is a bit of overkill, but friends of mine in the police department have told me a sufficient number of hair-raising tales of bad guys who get up after taking four or five .38 rounds, that I prefer to have an extra edge. If I have to shoot someone, I want him to go down and stay down.

In the bathroom I took a Contac and two aspirin, gargled, and decided I might live until bedtime. But not if it was too far away. I palpated my glands gently and winced. Where had this

24

bug come from? Just for insurance, I swallowed a handful of Vitamin C capsules. Linus Pauling might well be right.

I maneuvered by ancient MG into the tail end of commuter traffic and drove through the drizzling dusk to the television studio. Not quite seven o'clock. I wanted to be there when Valerie left. I had seen her drive away in a white Porsche, so I figured she wouldn't be too hard to find. She wasn't. I parked on the street, outside the studio lot, and watched. In a few minutes Valerie and about a dozen other people came out a side exit. She took a few minutes to reach her car, find the keys, and heave purse and briefcase into the back seat. I started the MG and slipped in behind her as she left the lot. Her license was one of those vanity plates. VAL, it said. Discreet. I wondered if her lover had given it to her.

For six or seven blocks I stayed a few car lengths behind her, not really thinking anything would happen. So when an old Buick wagon passed me and pulled in between us, I was surprised. I jotted down the license number on the back of a McDonald's napkin, settled back, and waited. The three of us drove around the park, through the University grounds, and into the Uplands Estates condominiums on Cedar Hill Crossroads. Valerie turned right onto Arbutus and the Buick followed. I went down one to Dogwood, turned right, and right again to bring me back onto Arbutus. Valerie's car was just pulling into the driveway of number 163. The Buick crawled past the house and stopped at the corner. It was now fully dark.

I passed the Buick at the corner stop sign and noted two young men, both white and clean shaven, one with sandy longish hair and glasses, one with short brown curls. Brown hair was lighting a cigarette as I passed the car, and I got a pretty good look at both of them as the match flared. They drove off toward the campus. I briefly debated the wisdom of following them, but time was pressing.

At the local McDonald's I ordered a chocolate milkshake. It seemed to help my sore throat. I sat in the car until seven-fifty, sipping it, then drove the short distance back to the condominiums. The black silhouettes of bare-branched Gary Oaks loomed like monstrous skeletons against the darker sky, and I shivered a little as I walked up the sidewalk. Valerie let me in, looking curiously at the paper bag in my hands.

"Tape recorder," I said, and she smiled nervously. She was dressed in a pair of jeans that looked as if they had cost a hundred bucks, and a pale blue V-neck sweater with an alligator logo on one breast. She ran a hand through her hair and motioned me into the house.

There was a woman sitting at one end of the sofa, and in the light of a small table lamp I recognized her at once. Well, things could have been worse—she could have been Princess Diana, or Madonna, or Margaret Thatcher. She was Tonia Konig, feminist, outspoken writer and speaker, and faculty member of the University's Women's Studies Department. A very public figure. What a mess.

Tonia looked at me belligerently. No Calvin Klein jeans and Izod sweaters for her. No sirree. She had on well-washed Levis, sneakers, and an old navy sweatshirt with the sleeves pushed up well past her elbows. She gave me a glare of baffled rage, then looked past me to Valerie.

"Tonia, this is Caitlin Reece," Valerie said. "Tonia doesn't think I should have hired you," she told me somewhat apologetically.

"I thought I detected a certain lack of enthusiasm," I replied. "Who do you know who owns a Buick wagon, dark green, late seventies model, license BNN eight-eight-seven?"

That gave them something to think about. They looked at each other, then me.

"Why?" Tonia asked flatly, not giving an inch.

"They followed Valerie home from work tonight. I followed them."

"I didn't notice anyone," Valerie said diffidently.

"Don't be hard so on yourself, " I said, "you weren't looking for them. I picked you up at the studio lot. They fell in behind you a few blocks later. Why was I there? Just a hunch."

Tonia made a disgusted sound and got up to pace a little. I looked at her, she looked at me, and I thought: Here's trouble we don't need.

Her pacing brought her to a spot in front of me, and I tried to stand a little taller. In her sneakers she had at least three inches on me. She flared her nostrils, reminding me of an Arabian horse. But there was nothing horsey about Tonia Konig. Shiny black hair, smoky blue eyes, Katherine Hepburn cheekbones, flawless complexion. She could have made big money with her face. When she didn't scowl, it was positively beautiful. At the moment, however, she was scowling ferociously, the glare she was giving me laser-like. She was the kind of woman my mother said could chew nails and spit battleships. Tough. Maybe as tough as me. But I was getting a little fed up with being the recipient of her foul looks. I was on her side.

"I'm Tonia Konig," she said finally, crossing her arms and leaning against the fireplace. She did not offer me her hand.

"I know," I informed her, not offering my hand either. Two could play this game. "I've seen you interviewed on television. I even started to read your book *A World Without Violence.*"

That clearly surprised her. She blinked several times, perhaps elevating me from the ranks of the functionally illiterate. Maybe there was hope for me yet in the good Dr. Konig's eyes. I tried not to let it go to my head.

"Started?" she asked suspiciously.

"Mmhmm. But I couldn't figure out how to apply the theory. It seemed kind of irrelevant to my line of work."

She actually snorted, and looked over at Valerie, who had collapsed on the couch. Valerie shrugged helplessly.

"I can see we have a difference of opinion here," I began.

"Why—" Tonia said.

"She—" Valerie interrupted.

I held up my hands. "I think I can summarize our differences."

Tonia exhaled sharply. Valerie nodded.

I continued, "Tonia would prefer to have Henry Kissinger or maybe Jesse Jackson do the job, seeing as how Gandhi is dead. Valerie, on the other hand, doesn't give a damn who does it as long as it gets done efficiently and discreetly. Knowing your divergent philosophies, Virginia Silver recommended me."

"Don't you dare patronize me, you little thug," Tonia said in a sub-zero voice.

"Oh God," Valerie muttered, raking her hair.

"I'm not patronizing you," I told Tonia. "Believe me, I have nothing but respect for your work. But I have to tell you that none of your theories, nothing you believe in, is going to do you a damned bit of good with this."

Tonia pressed her lips together, then shook her head. "I can't accept that," she stated. "Because if it were true, it would repudiate my life's work. Negate everything I stand for."

There was nothing I could say to make the pill go down more easily, even if I'd wanted to. She sat on the couch, crossed her arms, and glared.

"Oh, my God," Valerie said irrelevantly. "Caitlin, what must you think of us? Please come and sit down. Would you like to have a drink?" Playing hostess seemed suddenly important to her. I agreed and she scurried away to the kitchen.

"Aren't you a little . . . redundant?" Tonia asked me when we were alone. "We do have the criminal justice system, after all."

I smiled a little, looking away.

"But it's not good enough for you, is that it? What are you—a latter-day vigilante? Administering punishment to those who've escaped their just deserts?"

"Or never got them," I added. "I prefer to think of myself as complementary to the justice system. An adjunct."

She scowled disapprovingly. "What exactly *do* you do?"

"Deprive the predators of their prey. Intervene. Rescue. Recover. Interdict. Thwart. Deny the vultures their carrion. In plain English, render assistance to those who ask it of me. Like you did."

"I didn't ask you," she reminded me. "Val did. And I fail to see the difference between you and the predators."

I raised my eyebrows, but said nothing.

"What dictates how far you go in your . . . work?" she asked.

I thought I understood what she was getting at. "Nothing but my own discretion," I said.

That didn't seem to please her much. I had a pretty fair idea of what she thought of my moral attributes.

"But who decides on the merits of the victims' requests? And how do they find you?"

"I decide," I told her. "And they find me by making a phone call. The number is given to them by one of my satisfied ex-clients."

She was clearly as fascinated as she was repelled. "So you perform the moral triage," she said, sounding smug. "Make the diagnosis and do the surgery, too."

"A neat analogy," I commented. "Yeah, that's about it."

"Why you?" she demanded. "Do you have special abilities? Are you a crack shot, a black belt in karate, a moral philosopher, a—"

"No," I interrupted. "None of those things. But I do have the will. And the power. And it has nothing to do with physical strength or proficiency with weapons. It's a . . . determination." I broke off, unwilling to try to explain further.

"And you just woke up one morning and decided to do this?"

I thought my answer over carefully. How could I explain how frightened I was when I first began? And that my fear was a fear of believing in something again. Of caring. Of failing. But greater than the fear of trying and failing was the fear of not trying at all. For I had no wish to live in a world where no one tried. "Sort of," I equivocated.

Tonia shook her head in disbelief.

Valerie emerged from the kitchen where she had evidently been lurking, waiting for Tonia's moral objections to be aired. She passed around beer and glasses, and I drank mine from the can, conscious of my new image as a thug.

"Your proposed solution to problems is very unimaginative," Tonia told me, "and clearly a product of the paternalistic bureaucracy for which you worked for so long. The cycle of violence *can* be broken," she said earnestly. "History is full of encouraging examples. We're rational beings. It's so short-sighted to assume violence is the only method of settling disputes."

I felt sorry for her, and sorry for myself. A thug, she had called me. Well, maybe I was. "Violence works," I told her bluntly.

She looked at me as if I had crawled out from under a rock. "There are other ways," she said frostily. "And in this particular situation I don't like the fact that we're not even considering them."

"Tonia, with these kinds of people, there are no effective 'other ways.' Violence is the only choice."

She recoiled as though I had slapped her. Well, maybe it was distasteful, but I thought she needed to hear it.

"These are not the kinds of people you would want to sit down and reason with," I told her. "These are the inhabitants of the world's id. They're scum. As well as being economic opportunists, they're psychic vampires. They exploit decent people like you and Valerie, people they know can't strike back, and enjoy themselves while they're doing it. Other ways? There are none. The only language they speak is violence. I'd have been dead half a dozen times over if I'd tried anything else. I'm sorry if that offends your principles, but that's the way it is. And that's why I couldn't finish *A World Without Violence*."

"You enjoy it, don't you?" Tonia accused me after a moment.

I didn't flinch. "Yeah, I do. Scaring people half to death, breaking their bones, shooting them—I don't enjoy those acts. But I do enjoy outmaneuvering them. Thwarting them. Making them go away and stay away. I enjoy that a whole lot. And I enjoy the looks on their victims' faces when I tell them it's all over. I enjoy seeing good people happy again."

Her eyes slid away from mine, and I knew that I had scored some kind of victory. Just which kind, I wasn't sure. But it didn't make me feel good, because part of what I had told her was a lie. Sometimes, I *did* enjoy the scaring, breaking, and shooting. Sometimes, seeing a look of abject terror come into some pimple-faced punk's eyes, and knowing it was I, not he, who had the power— and that *he knew it* — was enjoyable in itself. And it scared the hell out of me.

I looked at my watch. Eight-forty. I sighed. "Look, feel free to hire someone else. Or to deal with this yourselves. Maybe I'm wrong. Maybe you can reason with these guys. Maybe—"

"Stop!" Valerie said. "Tonia isn't the only one who counts here. This is my life, too, and I'm not so morally fastidious."

Tonia closed her eyes. "You're right," she said after a moment. "We're in this together. If it were only I, I would act differently. But it isn't." She looked over at me. "I don't agree with your methods. But . . . " she pursed her lips as though the next words hurt her, "I agree that you should do what you can to help us."

* * * * *

It took only a minute to set up my equipment. I attached the microphone to the phone, plugged it into the recorder, rewound the tape, and we were ready.

"When they call," I told them, "don't panic, no matter what they say. Although it wouldn't hurt to seem a bit frightened. Just listen and agree to whatever their demands are." They looked at me in surprise. "You're not paying them a penny," I reminded them. "And we're going to get the letters back. So sound cowed and compliant. Okay?"

They nodded. I felt like the coach of a losing basketball team at half-time. Never mind, girls: they may be ahead of us 43-19, but we can still whip their asses. Get out there and fight! Well, maybe God would be on the side of the good guys this time. She sometimes was.

The phone rang promptly at nine o'clock. I motioned for one of them to pick it up, and started the recorder. To my surprise, Tonia, not Val, answered the phone. I picked up the dining room extension.

"Yes," she said coolly. To her credit, her voice didn't quaver.

"How are you tonight, Dr. Konig?" a strange, tenor voice inquired. I was a little surprised that he could identify Tonia.

Tonia looked across the room at me. I nodded. "I'm here," she told him coldly.

"That's good. That's real good. And have you and Ms. Newscaster Dyke thought over what we said in our note?"

Tonia gripped the phone so tightly her knuckles showed white. "Yes."

"Not too friendly, are you? But we know why that is, don't we?" the voice snickered. "You don't like men. Never mind, though. You're going to like us a whole lot before this is all over. So, what about it? Do we have a deal?"

"Yes," Tonia answered in a strangled voice. "We have a deal. We'll pay."

"Atta girl," the voice replied, loving every minute of Tonia's discomfort. "So here's what you'll do. We want five thousand dollars now, and a thousand a week after that."

"A thousand a week? For twenty-seven weeks? That's a fortune!"

"It is, isn't it?"

"So what's the five thousand dollars for?" Tonia demanded angrily. "What does that buy?" Her indignation was clearly real. God, how the blackmailer must be enjoying this.

"It buys my good will. And that's something you want to have, lady. Oh, yes."

Tonia glanced up at me, and I saw understanding in her eyes. Thug or not, I had been right. "It will take us a little while to raise that kind of money," she told the caller. "Neither of us has that much free cash."

"So get it," the voice said. "Take out a loan. Sell something. Write a book. Just make sure you have it by Saturday afternoon."

"Assuming we can get it, then what?"

"Oh, you'll get it if you know what's good for you. We'll phone at noon sharp. You'll be told where to bring it."

"All right."

"And listen, Dr. Dyke, don't even think about the police. They're not too crazy about your kind of women either, you know."

"There'll be no police."

"Good girl. We wouldn't want to see those steamy letters published in *The Mirror*, now would we?" More snickers. "Just wait for our call, Dr. K." The line went dead.

Tonia slammed the phone down. I hung up the extension and shut off the recorder.

"Let me hear it," Valerie said. I played the tape for her. "Son of a bitch," she whispered as the tape ended. "That son of a bitch!"

"We'd better talk about this," I told them. "Now, if possible."

Valerie sat down as if her legs had been pulled out from under her. Tonia paced around a little, then took off upstairs. "I'm getting the notes," she called from the hallway.

* * * * *

The notes had come in large brown envelopes—about 10 x 15, and both envelopes had come from the same package. There was a little dimple in the upper left-hand corner of each, as if something very heavy and sharp had sat on top of the package. And both notes seemed to be originals. I held the paper up to the light — expensive watermarked bond.

"What bad girls you've been!" the notes began with a kind of sick heartiness. "I've got some of your purple prose. Or is it lavender? Anyway, you'll definitely want these letters back. Attached is a sample, for verification. I'll call Monday at 8:00 p.m. to let you know how you can keep this sick little secret to yourselves. I think buying them back at a page a week is a good idea, don't you? You'll have 27 weeks to think about how naughty you've been. Until Monday."

Attached to the note was a photocopy of the final page of a handwritten letter. Signed by Tonia.

The more I thought about it, the chillier the back of my neck became. This was no ordinary blackmail note—this was one that had been written by a real macho woman-hater. That's not a contradiction in terms—I've met more of them than I care to recall. Sure, they preen and primp, and pump up their muscles, and read *Hustler* and *Screw*, and seek out fluffy young blonde things at singles bars. But underneath that macho facade lurks something else. A deeply felt dislike for and suspicion of women. A contempt. Gynophobia, the psychologists call it. Oh, these men have uses for women, no doubt about that, but they just don't *like* them. And the author of the blackmail note was one of these misogynists—I was certain of it. Worse still, he was a homophobe. A very dangerous combination. My years in the CP's office had taught me that.

I handed the papers back to Tonia. "Could I have some coffee?" I asked. "We're going to be at this awhile, and my decongestant is putting me to sleep."

Valerie disappeared into the kitchen, and in a few minutes I smelled coffee perking.

"How did the blackmailer get your letters?" I asked Tonia.

She shrugged. "A burglary. Just after Valentine's Day. I was away in Toronto then. They only took my television, stereo, and computer. At least I thought that's all they'd taken until I got this note."

"Where were the letters?"

"In a small wooden chest on a bookshelf in my bedroom."

"Did they make a mess? Were any drawers emptied?"

She nodded. "A few. And some books were thrown on the floor, but that was all."

"Interesting," I commented. "Did you call the police?"

"Oh yes. They came and took down the serial numbers of the stolen goods. But I've never heard from them since."

Valerie returned with coffee and cups on a tray. We helped ourselves.

Something that didn't make sense was nibbling at the back of my mind. It took a little nip, and I sat up straight. "How did these burglars happen to get so lucky as to get all the letters?" I asked.

"What do you mean?" Tonia said.

"All. Both sets. Tonia to Val and Val to Tonia. Usually people have in their possession only letters they've received. Not letters they've written."

They exchanged looks, and Valerie put down her coffee cup. "I suppose I'll have to tell you," she conceded. I braced myself. What else could there be?

"This isn't my house," she said. "It's Tonia's. I just . . . spend time here."

I held my breath. Something worse was coming. I would have bet money on it.

"I'm married," she told me, looking sidelong at Tonia. "My husband doesn't know about Tonia. Or about me."

I closed my eyes. It was getting worse by the minute.

"I left my letters here. With Tonia's. We thought it was best."

"Who is this husband?" I asked Valerie.

She looked apologetically at Tonia who stared fixedly at a spot on the carpet. I gathered this was not exactly Tonia's favorite topic of conversation. "His name is Baxter Buchanan. He's a . . . politician. A member of the legislative assembly—an MLA."

So? Why was she so frightened of him? He wasn't Satan, after all. "I don't get it. What would happen if he found out?" I asked Valerie. "It doesn't sound like you have a terrific marriage anyhow."

She looked embarrassed. "I haven't. But Baxter is so damned possessive. And passionate. He just can't accept that I want to leave him. God, I've been wanting to leave for years! It's just been in the past eighteen months or so, since my career has taken off, and since I met Tonia, that I've been determined to go. But he won't listen."

"So, let him listen to your lawyer," I suggested.

36

"Not right now," Valerie said firmly. "I'm in contract negotiations at the studio. My ratings are high. I don't need any problems."

"And Baxter would do that—make trouble for you at the studio?"

"Oh, yes," Valerie said fervently. "And more."

"More? What more?"

Valerie shook her head. "You'll just think I'm being melodramatic."

"Try me."

"He's told me that he'll never let me go," she said shamefacedly. "That he'd never let anyone else have me. Never." She shuddered. "He's insanely jealous. I can't imagine what he'd do if he found out that I wanted to leave him."

"I can't imagine either," I told her truthfully. "But things like this happen every day. You're not serving a life sentence, you know. C'mon, Val, what *would* he do? Curse and swear? Trash the house? Beat on you?"

She shook her head. Obviously any further speculation on the subject was *verboten.* At least for tonight.

"Okay," I told her. "Baxter Buchanan won't find out about the letters from me, so you don't have anything to worry about. Now let's discuss what we're going to do to get them back."

Val brightened a little at this.

"We have a couple of days until the money is due. In fact, almost a week. Let's make good use of them. I want to see where you both work. Who you come in contact with. That sort of thing."

"I have a class at eleven tomorrow morning," Tonia offered. "Theories of Conflict Resolution. Then I have a graduate seminar at one o'clock, and office hours from two to five."

"Okay. I'll meet Tonia in class at eleven, then come by the studio tomorrow afternoon after two to see you, Valerie."

Tonia frowned. "Is this really necessary? The students in my eleven o'clock class are mostly women, and well, they're kids."

"Yeah, it is necessary," I said. "Women too—even young ones—have been known to be criminals. And my job would sure be a lot easier if you let me do it my way."

Tonia bristled and made a sort of snorting sound. Valerie closed her eyes.

"And before tomorrow, there's some homework you two can do for me. Write out a list of your friends, acquaintances, relatives, enemies, cleaning ladies, gardeners, mechanics, hairdressers—anyone you see often. I'll need addresses and phone numbers, too." I stood up. That should keep them busy until at least midnight. "Until tomorrow then," I said. "Where do I meet you, Tonia?"

She glared. "Nootka Hall."

"See you then," I told her.

* * * * *

Soaking in a hot bath, a glass of Bailey's Irish Cream at hand, I thought over the mess Valerie and Tonia found themselves in. Although it seemed to me that Val was in a much bigger mess than Tonia. Her fear of the possessive Baxter was almost palpable. That, combined with the guilt she felt at her affair with Tonia, was enough to drive anyone a little crazy. Under the circumstances, she was holding up pretty well. I wasn't clear on what Tonia's attitude was, but I had a feeling she was going to be much more sensible about this than Val.

I dozed for a few minutes, then turned my mind to the burglary itself. From what Tonia had said, it hadn't seemed to be a very professional job. Burglars usually make one hell of a mess, and leave no drawer unturned, so to speak. And maybe that was the biggest thing we had going for us. If the culprits were amateurs at burglary, maybe they were amateurs at blackmail. Maybe they could be scared off. But with thousands of dollars at stake?

The more I thought about the blackmailer's note and his conversation tonight, the more I became convinced of something—whoever was behind this really had his heart in it. He was enjoying himself. The money was secondary. And that made him both easier and harder to deal with. Easier because he probably wasn't a professional, and might not have covered his tracks very well. And harder because he wasn't likely to listen to reason. Fanatics seldom do. And how many bad guys were involved in this, anyhow? The voice on the phone had identified himself as "we." I had to take him at his word. So there were at least two fanatical burglars/blackmailers. Oh goody.

I finished the Bailey's, took some more aspirins, towelled myself dry, and went to bed. Just as I was dozing off, a small furry body burrowed its way under the covers and down to my feet.

"Mrrank," he said politely.

It was nice to be needed. Even for my body heat. "Yeah," I said to Repo, stroking him with my foot, "goodnight to you, too."

TUESDAY

Chapter 4

The phone rang at exactly seven-fifteen the next morning. "Yes?" I inquired grumpily. Morning is not my favorite time of day. My lips don't even know they belong to me until after one cup of coffee.

"Ah, the hard-working consultant is up," a cheery masculine voice said. "We heard you come in late last night, and figured your clients must be taking advantage of you again. Why don't you come up for breakfast?"

"Aaargh," I said, clearing my throat, which felt as though Repo had been using it for a scratching post. "I don't think so. I feel like hell—I'm getting a cold. I think I'll just malinger here awhile."

"A cold?" Malcolm inquired with great interest, and I was immediately sorry I'd mentioned it. "Yvonne will make something to take care of *that*. Come on, Caitlin. What have you got to lose except your cold, hmm?"

I sighed. Oh, what the hell. I was awake. And besides, Repo had already deserted me. "Okay," I said. "But you'll have to take me as I am. I have to go to the University later, and I don't intend to get dressed until then."

"We'll put the tea on," Malcolm said.

I staggered upright, shoved my feet into my old Nikes, and lumbered to the bathroom. The mirror showed that I was indeed a mess: my grey sweat pants and my washed-out blue sweatshirt were old, faded, and mismatched; my hair looked like a thatched hut; and my red-rimmed eyes would have landed me a part in any Dracula movie. I ran my tongue over my furry teeth, and shuddered. God, imagine going through life as a tongue. I brushed my teeth, splashed some water on my face, and ran a comb through my hair.

Upstairs, Repo was happily purring in a pool of butterscotch sunshine in Malcolm's kitchen window. Malcolm, whistling *In An English Country Garden*, was busy in the greenhouse nipping or pinching or committing other acts of botanical violence. Yvonne was measuring out tea at the counter. The apartment smelled of cinnamon and mint, and exuded an aura of peace. I sighed.

"Morning, Caitlin," she said, examining me closely. "You look terrible. Too much coffee and red meat."

I groaned. It was too early in the morning for a debate on the merits of good clean living. I suspected that my case was hopeless, anyhow.

"Here," Yvonne said, handing me a mug of something hot and steaming. I took a tentative swallow. It was vaguely minty, with a not unpleasant oily undertaste. Experience had taught me not to inquire about the composition of Yvonne's concoctions. They worked.

44

Both Malcolm and Yvonne were blond, blue-eyed, and healthy. Their complexions glowed. Their teeth were white. They were never sick. So, on the off chance that there just might be some merit to all this natural living claptrap, I consented to letting them feed me whenever they were so inclined. Never let it be said that I don't have an open mind. And the arrangement seemed to suit everyone—they sensed a convert, and I scarcely ever had to cook. I finished the concoction and set the mug down on the table.

"How's business?" I asked.

Yvonne smiled happily. "Better and better. You know, Caitlin, we'll be able to repay your three thousand well before the note's due. In a month, I think. Putting the little restaurant in the back of the store was the best thing we ever did. You were a genius to think of it." She set a plate of blueberry and grain pancakes in front of me. "A physical wreck, but a genius."

"Where's *your* breakfast?" I inquired. "And what's Malcolm doing in there? Have the plants finally pinched back?"

"We've already eaten," she told me. "We just wanted to make sure that you did. Malcolm will be in in a minute. We'll all have some tea together before we go off to the store."

"Mmhmm," I said enigmatically, wolfing down my pancakes. I had no intentions of telling Yvonne about the delicious fare that the local McDonald's serves. Of which I had been intending to partake on my way to the campus. It would be like admitting to Van Gogh that you liked cartoons. "Delicious," I said truthfully.

Yvonne beamed, and got up to make tea.

"Well, well," Malcolm said from behind me. "The ailing Caitlin Reece. We may save you yet." He planted a quick kiss on my cheek.

"Don't bet on it, buster," I told him. "I'm past redemption. Yvonne keeps trying, but . . . " I shrugged. "It's

45

my rotten lifestyle that's at the root of it all. And my unregeneracy."

"Yeah, right," Malcolm said. "If it weren't for you, we might still be struggling to make ends meet. Whatever you do for a living, we're grateful."

Malcolm and Yvonne think I'm a business consultant. And in some ways, they're right. I've never seen the point of explaining to them what I really do. I crossed my arms and sat back in my chair, waiting. Malcolm and Yvonne weren't the type to ask for a loan—I'd had to offer to finance their business expansion in the first place. They're hard workers, and had located their health food store in a choice location. All they needed was a little help to really make the business profitable. Now that they had begun to be wildly successful, it embarrassed them. Worse yet, they were financial idiots. But they'd mentioned money twice. I wondered what was up.

"Caitlin," Malcolm began, "we don't know much about money."

I tried my best not to smile.

He looked over at Yvonne for moral support. She nodded. "Um, well, there's this man. He comes into the store quite often. He seems like a nice person. And he seems to share a lot of our ideals," Malcolm said.

I sighed. "So what does he want you to invest in?"

Malcolm goggled. Yvonne came over with the teapot and sat down.

"I told you we should ask her!" she said to Malcolm. "We didn't want to bother you," she told me apologetically, "but we really could use your advice. It's a sort of fund," Yvonne began. She looked at me in wonder. "But how did you know?"

I shook my head. Better not to tell them. "Just a good guess. So tell me about the fund." I looked at them in alarm. "You haven't given this guy any money yet, have you?"

"No." Malcolm looked over at Yvonne. "Not yet."

"Thank God. The fund, Malcolm. Tell me."

"Oh yeah. Well, he said it's a pool of investors like us—mostly people in small businesses. People who have strong moral positions. You know that we don't stock cosmetics that are tested on animals, and so on. Well, he takes people's money and finds ethical investments for them. Investments that we wouldn't necessarily know about."

I shook my head. Babes in the woods. "Did he leave any literature?"

"Well, no," Malcolm admitted. "But he showed us a list of companies, and explained to us what they did. It sounded fine."

"But *I* said we should talk to you first," Yvonne told me. "You see, we plan to pay off your note next month, and then we'd have that payment free. We want to do something good for ourselves with it."

I nodded, barely restraining myself from telling this earnest, blue-eyed pair of dopes that they'd almost fallen for one of the oldest tricks in the con man's book. "I'm glad you came to me," I said calmly. "I might just know someone who can check out the fund. And the guy who runs it, too. Did he leave a card?"

Yvonne nodded, and took it out of a pocket of her sweater. I put it down beside my tea mug. "His name's Oliver Renbo," she said. "The fund is called the Rainbow Fund."

"I'll take care of it," I told them. "Don't worry."

They smiled at each other, immensely relieved, and Yvonne poured tea.

"When does this guy usually come into the store?" I asked, sipping the aromatic brew.

"Just after two. After the markets are closed, he says. After he's gotten the day's quotes."

The markets, my eye. The closest he probably ever came to the financial markets was to wrap his garbage in the business section of the *Victoria Times Colonist*. I could hardly wait to talk to this fund manager. But first things first. I finished my tea, and stood up.

"I'll let you know about this as soon as I can," I told them. "In the meantime, hold on to your checkbook."

They smiled sheepishly and nodded.

"Feel any better?" Yvonne asked, walking me to the door.

I swallowed. Amazingly, there was no sore throat. "I can't believe it," I told her. "I feel almost human."

She hugged me. "I don't know what we'd do without you," she said.

I disentangled myself and hurried downstairs with a lump in my throat.

As I would be making an appearance in the groves of academe, I decided to wear my freshly dry-cleaned brown slacks, a cheery yellow cotton shirt and vest, and my fawn camel hair blazer. Besides, the blazer had the advantage of hanging nicely over my gun. Like my American Express card, I never leave home without it. Over the years I've made quite a few people very angry with me, and I don't want to be caught off guard when the pigeons come home to roost, so to speak.

But don't misunderstand me—there are at least half a dozen things I'd rather try before shooting. As the Chinese proverb goes: "Of the thirty-six ways of avoiding danger, running away is best." I couldn't agree more. I don't kid myself for a minute that I could stand up and slug it out with some two-hundred pound man, even though I know all the right places to attack. One lucky punch and it would be all over for me. Have you ever been *hit* by a two-hundred pound man? I was, once, and I thought I'd been knocked into the next county. My ears rang for a week. Now I don't let the bad guys get that close. If I can't scare them off, and I can't run away, I have that irresistible voice of reason, the .357 Magnum. Smith and Wesson are very persuasive. Tonia would be horrified, I mused. Tough.

48

I found a place for my MG in the visitor's lot and walked along under the oaks and evergreens to Nootka Hall. April is a fickle month on the coast, and the watery sun seemed undecided today. Well, I could forgive it. I didn't feel too decisive myself. My throat didn't hurt, but my eyes felt hot and scratchy. Colds are such a pain in the butt. I'd rather be down and out for a day or two—real, genuine, prostrate-in-my-bed sick—than this miserable business of not being sick enough to go to bed, but not being well enough to function properly.

The lecture theatre was empty when I went in. Tonia was at the front, fussing with some papers. Today she wore jeans, a forest green wool sweater, and a navy suede jacket. Her gleaming black hair was parted in the middle and tucked behind her ears. She wore no makeup, but with that fine complexion, who would bother?

"Morning," I said, taking a seat at the back. She glanced up from her notes and gave me a hostile look.

"Morning," she answered coldly. She took a sheaf of papers out of her briefcase and held them out to me. "Here are the names you wanted. It took us half the night to make the list," she said aggrievedly.

I hopped up, retrieved the papers, and returned to my seat. "Thanks," I told her. She ignored me.

As the lecture theatre filled, I looked around for the two characters I'd seen last night in the Buick wagon, but of course they weren't there. That would have been too easy. As Tonia had mentioned, the students were mostly women (the course was given under the aegis of the Women's Studies Department), although there were more men than I would have guessed. In fact, of the thirty-seven students in the class, I counted six men. And none of the students could exactly be called "kids."

The women were an interesting cross-section of the women's community, I observed. Flannel shirts and corduroy pants were much in evidence. I thought I recognized several of the women from my infrequent visits to the local women's coffee house or bookstore, but I couldn't be sure. Then there were the leftover flower children—long cotton skirts of some Indian design, several layers of hand-knit sweaters, hair long and flowing, or in braids, dreamy expressions. One wispy creature passed me in a cloud of Patchouli perfume, and I was immediately transported back to the late sixties and my own undergraduate days. I felt ancient. I looked around and identified several other aged crones like myself, and felt immensely better. One nattily dressed oldster seemed to be well into her fifties, I decided. Why, compared to her, I was a mere slip of a girl. I tried not to look smug.

Tonia looked up from her notes and the buzz of chatter ceased.

"Today I want to talk about the technique of nonviolent action," Tonia said.

I perked up. Nonviolent action—wasn't that a contraction in terms?

"Most people believe that military combat is the only effective way to wage social and political conflict. I disagree. Nonviolent action provides another approach. However, both the techniques of nonviolent action and the term itself have been the subject of many misconceptions."

She looked around the room. No one raised a hand. Pens were busy scribbling in notebooks. Aha, I thought, Dr. Konig was that almost extinct genre of academic, The Lecturer. She stood at the front of the room and talked, and the kids took down what they were able. I must confess, The Lecturer was my favorite sort of professor. I always loathed the seminars and discussion groups in which certain students were encouraged to bore the hell out of the rest of us with their opinions and insights. I always wondered how the insights of a nineteen-year-old could possibly be superior to those of a forty-year-old who has a Ph.D. in the subject and has been thinking about it for twenty years. I paid my money to hear

50

what the *professor* thought, not what my classmates thought. I was glad to see that Tonia brooked none of this class participation nonsense.

Strangely enough, her teaching methods seemed agreeable to the students. I sighed. Those awful days of the seventies were gone for good, I hoped. Students seemed to have returned to some degree of sanity.

"By using the term technique, I mean the overall method of conducting the struggle," Tonia continued. "Is the technique one of protest, demonstration, or so on. And by nonviolent action, I mean the specific method of protest, demonstration, noncooperation in which the actionists, *without employing physical violence*, refuse to do things which they are required to do, or do things which they are forbidden to do.

"Nonviolent action is a generic term. It includes the large class of phenomena variously called nonviolent resistance, Satyagraha, passive resistance, positive action, and nonviolent direct action. While it is not violent, it *is* action, and not inaction. Passivity, cowardice, and submission must be surmounted if it is to be used—it demands commitment, high moral fibre, and intelligence."

She looked directly at me, and I'm embarrassed to admit that I blushed. She made me feel small and inadequate. For only a moment. Then I was madder than hell.

"Nonviolent action is a means of conducting conflict and waging struggles and should not be equated with purely verbal dissent or solely psychological influence. It is not pacifism. It is not an escapist approach to the problem of violence, for it can be used against opponents relying on violent sanctions." She paused and looked around, but her glance did not include me this time. There were no questions. I found, to my surprise, that I wanted her to continue.

"Now, let's get specific," she said. "There is a very wide range of methods of nonviolent action. At least one hundred and twenty-five have been identified. They tend to fall into three classes—nonviolent protest, non-cooperation, and nonviolent intervention. Nonviolent protest is usually symbolic—marches, pilgrimages, picketing, vigils, public meetings, distribution of protest literature, and so on. Non-cooperation is a little more serious, and more likely to present the opponent with difficulties in maintaining the normal efficiency and operation of his system. Methods of non-cooperation include strikes, economic boycotts and embargoes, boycotts of elections, civil disobedience, and even mutiny. Nonviolent intervention challenges the opponent more directly, and assuming that fearlessness and discipline are maintained, relatively small numbers may have a disproportionately large impact. These include sit-ins, fasts, reverse strikes, nonviolent obstruction, nonviolent invasion, and parallel government."

"But of course," she continued, "selection of the method to be used must be done with care. The type of issue involved, the nature of the opponent—his aims and strengths, the type of counteraction he is likely to use, the depth of feeling in the general populace for the issue, and the degree of repression the actionists are likely to face. Just as in a military battle weapons are carefully selected, so also in nonviolent action the choice of specific methods is very important."

Despite my ire, I was impressed. I had dismissed her as a pantywaist go-limp-and-get-arrested type. Evidently I had been wrong. She sounded tough. But what she was talking about was theory. Wasn't it?

"And that brings me to your assignment," she told the class. "In recent history there have been dozens of cases of nonviolent action. Successful nonviolent action." She looked around and smiled. "Find them."

The class heaved a collective groan. Hands flew up. Tonia held up her own hand to ward off questions. "The University has an excellent microfilm library. Its newspaper file is quite complete. I suggest you divide yourselves into groups and proceed from there. That's all for today."

I tried to put aside my irritation at Tonia's comments regarding commitment, high moral fibre, and intelligence. After all, what did I care what she thought of me? The students left in a rush, presumably to zero in on all that microfilm, and I hurried to catch Tonia at the doorway. She looked at me wearily.

"Do we really have to do this?"

"I do," I told her. "I thought we hashed all that out last night." No response. "If you like, I can trail three paces behind like Prince Philip."

"Oh come on," she snapped. "And stop playing the fool."

"I can't promise anything so rash," I told her cheerfully. "We no-moral-fibre types are like that."

She shook her head and strode out into the April sunshine, me at her elbow.

"I was interested in what you had to say about nonviolent action," I told her seriously, thinking to try to patch up our differences.

"Please," she said frostily. "Don't insult yourself by trying to make polite conversation on a subject so clearly foreign to you."

The question I had been about to ask concerning the Hungarian revolution froze on my lips. To hell with you, Konig, I decided. And I was angry at myself for having given her an opening through which to shoot another dart at me. Well, that's what you get for seeking enlightenment, Caitlin. Better stick to what you do best—being a thug.

Chapter 5

We were halfway across the park when I saw him coming. He was on roller skates and had one of those Sony Walkmans stuck on his ears. Weaving along the walkway in a world of his own, he managed nonetheless to avoid the few pedestrians in his path. But his seemingly artless zigs and zags bothered me. My antennae started to bristle. I looked around for somewhere to go, but the ground on either side of the flagstone path was soggy at best, and muddy at worst. I started to lead Tonia off the path, but she pulled away from me.

"What on earth *are* you doing?" she asked indignantly.

The skater turned on a dime, and he and Tonia went down on the soggy ground in a tangle of arms and legs, Tonia on the bottom. There were very few people around, I noted, as I took a handful of hair, another of jacket, and pulled him off her.

"Whaddya doing?" he screamed. With surprising agility he squirmed away, but I heaved him face down in the mud and put my boot on the back of his neck.

"Awfully clumsy, aren't you?" I said, and stomped a little. He bucked, trying to lever himself up, so I knelt on his back and yanked on his hair again. He yelped, but stopped bucking. "Keep your hands where I can see them. So what's your name?"

"Fuck off," he said heatedly.

Ah, the verbal bankruptcy of the young. Fuck, it seemed, was the only epithet they knew.

"Well, Mr. Off," I replied, reaching into his back pocket for his wallet, "I think I'll just extract a few dollars from you to pay for my friend's drycleaning." I couldn't have cared less about the money—what I wanted was to get a look at his identification. I flipped his wallet open, extracted his driver's license, student ID card, athletic pass, and a ten dollar bill, and threw the wallet into the bushes. All pieces of identification bore the names James Harrington. His driver's license said that he lived at 1074 Redfern Street. I threw the rest of his ID after the wallet. "Listen, you, I'm going to get up now." I looked over and saw that Tonia was now on her feet. Good. She looked a little dazed, and the back of her clothes were pretty muddy, but she seemed all right. "My friend and I are going to walk away. You are going to give us a few minutes, then you will retrieve your wallet from the bushes and skate off. In the other direction. Understand?"

"Yeah, yeah," he said indignantly. "I don't know what you're so steamed about. It was just an accident."

"Mmmhmm," I said, getting off him.

I took Tonia's arm and walked her out of the park. I looked back once and saw James Harrington scrabbling in the bushes. When I looked back again, he was nowhere in sight.

"Are you okay?" I asked Tonia.

She nodded. "He just knocked the wind out of me. Don't you think you overreacted, though? It did seem like an accident."

I shrugged. "It's possible, I suppose. But that kid had to do a turn Baryshnikov would be proud of in order to hit you."

She looked at me in surprise. "To hit me? But why?" Then comprehension dawned. "You don't think . . ."

"Maybe."

"Oh. But he's gone!" she said in frustration, looking around. "Now we'll never find out."

I smiled. "Oh yes we will. I got a look at his driver's license. I may even have a little chat with him later today. Don't worry. If he knows anything, he'll tell me."

She bristled. "You seem very sure of yourself."

"Well, let's just say I'm persuasive."

She looked at me suspiciously.

"Would you like to go somewhere and have a drink?" I suggested. She was looking a little white, I thought.

"Actually, yes," she said. "Maybe even a double."

* * * * *

Tonia finished off half of her double Scotch in one swallow. I was impressed. A serious drinker. "I want to know something about you," she asked me curiously.

"Oh? What?" I couldn't imagine what she could possibly find of interest about me, except whether I had dropped out of kindergarten or elementary school. My stock, I sensed, was not high with Tonia.

"How did you know to do what you did?"

I raised an eyebrow.

"Back there in the park. With that boy."

I took a careful swallow of my own Scotch, followed by a deep breath. "Practice." As I expected, she frowned.

57

"Practice," she repeated. She thought this over for a moment, then looked up at me. "Do you have to do a lot of that kind of thing?"

"You mean being nasty? Intimidating people?"

She nodded.

"Sometimes. Especially when people don't immediately tell me what I want to know. Extracting information is just a learned skill, after all." Why did I have the feeling that we were going to reprise last night's conversation? I knew already that she didn't like what I did. But she had agreed to accept it. Why couldn't she just let things lie?

"So you think of what you do as a skill?"

I took another sip of Scotch. "Of course. Instincts alone aren't good enough. The fine art of persuasion takes a long time to learn. Although it's probably a skill, not an art. Persuading people to do what you want takes a lot of trial and error to find out what methods work best. To find the things that people respond to. And then, you practice the methods." I shrugged. "That's it."

"You make it sound so easy," she said critically, "but we both know it can't be that easy. You're talking about using whatever methods the situation calls for to . . . persuade people. That's not persuasion. That's coercion. In some cases, violent coercion."

"That's right."

She finished her drink in silence.

I wanted to say something in my own defense, but nothing clever occurred to me. Well, if she wanted to think of me as a thug, she could go ahead and do that. I hadn't noticed her ask me not to use violent coercion on hers and Val's behalf, though. My crap detector vibrated. Did I detect a double standard here?

"Do you want to eat lunch?" I asked her. "There's a great little natural food cafe not too far from here. In fact, we could walk."

58

"Thanks," she said. "I would like to eat something. Although the temptation is to sit here and have a few more Scotches." She deftly extracted a couple of coins from her jacket pocket. No fumbling in handbags for her. "I think I'll cancel my class and my office hours this afternoon," she told me, fiddling with a dime. "You may find this quite laughable," she said, frowning at me belligerently, "but I'm beginning to feel a little, well, apprehensive."

"I don't find that laughable at all. They—whoever they are—clearly mean you to be frightened." I shrugged. "If I'd just been run down in the park, I might be frightened, too."

She bent forward intently. "But you're not, are you?"

I said nothing.

"Well, are you?"

"No."

* * * * *

Malcolm was obviously pleased to see me, and when he saw who I had with me, his pleasure turned to delight. I made introductions, and he found Tonia and me a seat by the window.

"The soups are always good here," I suggested.

Tonia nodded distractedly and when the waitress came to take our order we ordered black bean soup and whole grain bread. And tea.

Tonia tucked a stray wing of black hair behind her ear and looked at me. "This isn't the sort of place I would have thought you'd like."

I laughed a little. "The owners are my friends," I told her. "I'm prepared to make a few compromises for the sake of friendship."

She looked at me suspiciously, but the bean soup arrived just at that moment. We ate in silence.

59

I decided to go for the jugular. "I thought we'd decided last night to call a truce."

She blinked quickly a few times, then looked down into her soup. "Yes. We did."

"Well?"

She broke off a piece of her whole grain bread and nibbled on it thoughtfully. "I have to accept that what you do can achieve results," she conceded. "But I don't have to like it."

"Or me."

She shook her head. "Caitlin, you don't fit into my . . . world view. My system of beliefs. My theories."

"Do I have to? Surely not everything fits."

She looked at me steadily, blue eyes troubled. "Why shouldn't everything fit? God, I've spent enough time developing these theories. And until I met you, things did pretty well mesh."

I sighed. She had a problem. Because if she truly maintained that there was no place in conflict resolution for violence, she was in trouble. Her theories were about to be destroyed. Well, maybe I could give her a different perspective on her theories. At worst she could tell me to go to hell. I took a deep breath. "Perhaps you should look on this as professional development."

"Don't make foolish jokes," she said, glowering.

"I'm not," I protested. "Couldn't you think of this as opportunity to test your theories? A field experiment?"

That produced a disdainful look. Undaunted, I forged on.

"Theories have to be compared to real life sometime, don't they? And if they can't explain events, then the theory has to be amended." I shrugged. "That doesn't seem like the destruction of a life's work to me. It seems like common sense."

She looked at me inscrutably, neither agreeing nor disagreeing.

We finished our lunch, and I looked at my watch. "I have to go somewhere, and I want to know you're safe." I eyed her uncertainly. "Are you going to give me an argument about it?"

"No," she said unexpectedly. "Where do you have in mind that's safe?"

"Well, this place would do, but I don't know how long I'll be gone. So let's pick someplace no one knows about. My place. I'd like you to come home with me and stay put until I get back."

She considered this. "All right."

* * * * *

I was reasonably sure no one followed us by the time I pulled into the driveway at my house. Tonia hefted her briefcase and followed me inside.

"Oh," she said as I locked the front door and she went ahead into the living room.

I looked to see what the problem was, but she was just standing there in front of my bookcase. "Something wrong?"

"No," she answered absently, looking at the titles. "I was just startled to see so many books."

Well, she did have a point. I guess I have every book I've ever bought—thousands by now. I'm particularly fond of science fiction, and one wall is stuffed with books by Bradley, Niven and Pournelle, Asimov, Brin, LeGuin, Cherryh, Russ, and so on. My back copies of *Omni* (I have the inaugural issue) and *Analog* reside there, too. And in the section beside science fiction is my Shakespeare collection. I have about a dozen sets of the *Collected Works*, five or six editions of only the plays, and the same number of the sonnets. Then there are about a hundred works of criticism. I can't help it—I'm a Shakespeare buff.

Tonia took down one of my copies of the sonnets and leafed through it. "Do you know Sonnet One-Forty-Seven?" she asked me.

"Sure," I replied. "It's a problem for the critics. One of the Dark Lady sonnets, isn't it?"

She looked at me curiously. "Dark Lady?"

"Yeah. Some woman who apparently spurned Will's advances. Or was unfaithful. Or turned out to be a mere mortal. Although there's controversy over whether or not there was even a woman at all. His fondness for his patron was well known."

She replaced the book quickly and took down another. "Have you really read all this criticism?"

I smothered a smile. "Oh, well, not all of it. I'm working my way through the books slowly. You know, I read a little each night until I get tired of moving my lips."

She glared at me. "You like to do that, don't you?"

"Do what?" I inquired in feigned innocence.

"Perpetuate the image of the illiterate thug." She snorted. "It gives you some sort of perverse satisfaction."

I headed for the bedroom. "Yeah, that's me. Perverse."

She followed me and leaned against the door frame. "I think I've underestimated you. You're clearly a very complicated person." She looked a little sheepish. "Although you do make things difficult."

I eyed her curiously, took off my good camel hair jacket and pants, and hung them in the closet. "I'm not so complicated. Who says thugs can't read Shakespeare?"

I rummaged around for a pair of navy cotton pants, purloined from an earlier adventure, zipped them up, found a belt, and threaded it through my holster. I got it positioned where I wanted it in the small of my back, and took a navy jacket off a hanger. It had a large orange oval on the back that said METRO GAS and a smaller oval on the right breast that read SMYTHE.

"Your gun is showing," she said quietly.

I put on the jacket and zipped it up. "Now it isn't."

"Do you need to take it?" she asked curiously.

"Better safe than sorry," I told her truthfully, stuffing my hair up under a Metro Gas cap, donning a pair of mirror sunglasses, and sliding a clipboard under my arm.

She shook her head in dismay, turned and went back to the living room. I tried not to be irritated. Tough luck if she hadn't like what she'd just seen. Who asked her to watch me change anyhow? Nosy broad.

"Help yourself to coffee and donuts and so on," I told her. "I shouldn't be more than an hour or so."

"I hope not," she said. "I have to go home and get ready for a dinner party tonight." She gave me a long look. "Surely you're not going to want to . . . "

"Tag along?" I supplied. "It would probably be a good idea. Where is it?"

"At a colleague's house. There will be five of us."

"Hmm," I said, thinking. "Well, maybe I'll just follow you. To see that you get there and back without being run down by any more skaters."

She tapped her foot in irritation. "All right. But I think you're overreacting." A thought crossed her mind. "What about Val? We're in this mess together. Aren't you concerned that young hoodlums may be mugging her, too?"

"Yeah, I am. But I can't be in two places at once. I'll go see Val once you're safely partying." I walked to the door. "Oh, if a large grey cat comes to the window and hollers to get in, would you open it for him? And don't let him sweet-talk you. He doesn't need a thing to eat."

She actually smiled. Was it my feline ownership that amused her? Perhaps she had expected me to keep a brace of pit bulls. Or a tank of pirranhas. "I'll let him in. What's his name?"

I was embarrassed. "Repo. Short for Repossessed. The kids who live upstairs—the ones who run the health food store and cafe—gave him to me. They liberated him from some horrible sounding animal experiment at the University. He's definitely on his ninth life."

I was almost out the door when she said it. "I do hope you'll . . . be careful."

I felt like five-year-old Caitlin being sent off to school by Mom. "I always am," I told her a little acerbicly. "It's my edge."

Chapter 6

Redfern Street is just a few blocks from the Oak Bay Recreation Center, in a section of the municipality euphemistically called "Oak Bay Border." Realtors call it that to make it more saleable. Lying north of the so-called "Tweed Curtain" of Foul Bay Road, it is unacknowledged by us who live in Oak Bay proper. It is beyond The Pale. Actually, it is a perfectly ordinary mixed residential district of retired couples and young marrieds. The houses are small, plain, and modest, their yards neat. There are none of the astonishing Tudor monstrosities, towering oaks, elaborate gardens, and lush lawns, that you find in Oak Bay.

And in my opinion, Oak Bay is the nicest thing about Victoria. Pains have been taken by the merchants to make it appear the quintessential English village. The shop fronts are black and white Tudor, the lampposts sport baskets of flowers, and everyone knows everyone else. Within a space of three blocks we have all the necessities of life—a fishmarket, butcher shop, tea and coffee emporium, English woolen shop, a bakery, a hardware store, a tobacconist's, a shoe store, a travel agency, a delicatessen, a photo shop, several banks, two grocery stores, three tearooms, and a genuine British pub. Elderly ladies in Harris tweed skirts and sensible shoes march their Corgis and Westies enthusiastically up and down Oak Bay Avenue in all kinds of weather. It really does have a village atmosphere, and I loved it. I would never consider living on the other side of the Tweed Curtain.

Redfern Street in Oak Bay Border could have been a street in any city in Canada. But although many of the houses seemed in need of a spring fix-up or two, none was as seedy looking as James Harrington's. The neighborhood definitely didn't deserve him.

I left my car at the top of the block and walked to 1074—a frame two-story once white, with peeling porch, faschia, and eavestroughs. A chain link fence enclosed the yard. I immediately thought dog, and opened the gate cautiously. No slavering canine appeared, so I trotted up the steps and onto the porch and rang the bell. No answer. Just to be sure, I leaned on it for maybe a full minute, but no one appeared. I went back out the gate and down the driveway beside the house, looking for the meter. I found it on the far side of the house, on the back porch, which was every bit as scabrous as the front. I recorded a bunch of kilowattage on my clipboard, and picked the back door lock when I was sure no one could see me.

Opening the door a few inches, I waited to be sure a maddened Doberman wasn't tethered to the doorknob. Once inside, I found myself in what my grandmother would have called a mud room. There were hooks on one wall which held a grimy down vest, a denim jacket, and a raincoat. Against the far wall was an enormous cairn of beer cases. I figured this entrance was used only for moving the beer in and out. I took a toothpick out of my pocket, broke it, and jammed the pieces into the lock. Now the spring wouldn't release, and while the door would close, it wouldn't lock. I certainly didn't want to have to fumble with a locked door in case I needed to make a quick departure.

"Hello!" I yelled. "Anyone home?" Just your friendly meter reader come about a problem with your service. No answer. Besides, the place *felt* empty. I walked through a kitchen, surprisingly neat and tidy, and a living room furnished with two old flowered couches, a ratty-looking carpet remnant, and incongruously, a bookcase full of shiny electronic equipment. There was a new Onkyo stereo and speakers, two Sony Trinitrons, a Magnavox VCR, a Canon portable video camera and deck, and a couple of Sony Walkmans. A table by the window held an IBM PC computer, two Epson printers, one of the new Zenith portables, and an Apple Macintosh. Bingo. This place looked like a used electronics store. Could it be this easy? I quickly wrote down the serial numbers.

Now, upstairs, or downstairs? I ran upstairs. Two bedrooms, both furnished, one with bunk beds. Three people lived here. In the front bedroom a notebook on the desk said Lester Baines, Journalism 3. There was a Canon AE-1 camera and various lenses on the desk. I opened the drawers and quickly looked through them. Nothing much. Papers, journals, magazines, pens, pencils, empty film containers. The dresser held clean clothes, the closet mostly dirty ones. But a stack of cardboard file cabinets shoved in the closet proved interesting. I hauled one out into the room. It contained Lester's photography assignments, I supposed—some interesting shots of the campus, and some perfectly awful ones of tree bark and ocean waves. In the back, however, was a file stuck up at an angle as if it had been removed recently and shoved back in some haste. *Victor* it said. I pulled it out. It was full of pictures of people, obviously taken with a telephoto lens. Big deal. Another boring journalism assignment. I almost shoved it back when a photo fell out onto the floor. I picked it up to return it to the file folder and froze in mid-gesture. The photo was of Tonia.

She was standing at her kitchen sink, doing dishes, head turned, talking to someone. I flipped it over. On the back Lester had scribbled *Subject 29, Feb. 10*. I looked more closely at the file, and began to turn the pictures over. All the photos were candid shots of individuals, and all were labeled the same way, with subject and date notations. I began to get a bad feeling about all this. The negatives were clipped to the back of the file, and I hesitated for only a moment before I shoved them into a pocket. I returned the file to the box and the box to the closet, and hurried into the next bedroom, the one with bunk beds.

A quick search of the drawers and closet yielded no useful information save that this was the lair of the maladroit skater James Harrington, who was, it seemed, an engineering student. Harrington shared the room with another engineering student, Mark Jerome. Well, perhaps I had found enough for one day. I ran downstairs and exited the way I had entered, removing the broken toothpick from the lock.

On my way up the driveway I saw a dark green Buick wagon drive up in front of the house—the same car that had followed Val home from the studio. I recognized the license plate. Three young men got out—the two I had seen in the car the night before, and a third I recognized as James Harrington. But the driver was new to me. He was about fifty, maybe five-eight, stocky build, porcine features, grey crewcut, and mean little pale eyes. The kids' fence? Maybe.

I touched my cap to them and crossed the street. None of them even looked at me twice. Wear a uniform and carry a clipboard and you can go anywhere.

* * * * *

On my way home, I mulled over the photos I had found in Lester Baines' files. Why were his photos of people labeled with subject names and dates? Perhaps my intuition was wrong—perhaps this was just another journalism assignment. I doubted it, though. And who was Victor? Well, that was one problem. The other was the electronic gear I had found in the house. Was this really what it seemed—a trio of enterprising kids running a burglary ring? Was the older man I'd seen with them really a fence? Or their Fagin? Should I care? I decided I didn't have enough information even to guess. Yet. Well, maybe when the negatives were developed, I'd have more to go on.

I drove to the Oak Bay photo shop, put a rush on the negatives, and dashed across the street to the Back Alley Deli. The owners made the best muffins in the world. I bought half a dozen, a hunk of cheddar, a quarter pound of shaved ham, and ran back to the car. Maybe I could get this stuff smuggled into the house and devoured without Yvonne's finding out. I intended to try.

Back on Monterey, everything looked all right as I pulled into the driveway and parked. I rang the bell and Tonia let me in, checking me out first through the little window in the door.

She had drawn the curtains, and turned on a table lamp. Was it that late? I looked at my watch. Nearly five-thirty.

There was a mohair blanket on the couch with a grey tail protruding from under it and I guessed that Tonia and Repo had been snuggling together. I felt envious, and realized with a start that it wasn't envy of Tonia. Heck, I could snuggle up to Repo any old time. Tonia turned to look at me and I noted that her hair was mussed, and her eyes still a little unfocussed from sleep. She closed her eyes and stretched, her lean body arching in an unconsciously graceful catlike motion, and I checked an impulse to reach out and smooth her hair.

Good grief, Caitlin, get a grip on yourself, I told myself. Going to the kitchen for a drink suddenly seemed like a pretty good idea, and I quickly hustled my overactive libido out of the room and temptation's path. I felt certain that Tonia would be able to tell how rapidly I had progressed from thoughts of hair smoothing to thoughts of earlobe nibbling. I decided to restrict all such activities to the shaved ham.

My throat had begun to feel raspy again, and I suspected that another shot of Yvonne's concoction was in order. Well, a handful of vitamin C and a drink would have to suffice.

"How did the meter reading go?" Tonia asked from behind me.

"Good. Meters are amazing things. You can learn a lot from them," I equivocated, deciding not to tell her about the pictures I had found until I had some idea what they meant. And right now, I had a paucity of good ideas. I resisted turning around to look at her, and poured myself a Scotch. "Want a drink?" I called over my shoulder. I swallowed a healthy belt, along with my lustful thoughts of the good Dr. Konig, and turned around.

"No thanks." Tonia leaned against the kitchen door frame, arms crossed. Her dark green sweater clung softly to her breasts. "You haven't forgotten?"

"Forgotten what?"

She closed her eyes wearily. Well, what could you expect from a thug? "My dinner party."

"Of course not," I lied. "Just fortifying myself." Inwardly, I cursed. What I really wanted was a hot bath and my bed. Or a cold shower and my bed. Instead I could look forward to an evening spent lurking in my car, waiting for Tonia. Great. Well, that would cool my ardor. And I could kill some of the time going to see Val. "Ready when you are," I told her, tossing Smythe's jacket over one of the kitchen chairs and exchanging it for my heavy suede windbreaker.

Tonia gave me a long, unreadable look as I zipped up, and I tried my best to think about anything but her earlobes. I mentally whizzed through two verses of "Jabberwocky" and had just come to the line about the frumious Bandersnatch when She turned away. I exhaled heavily, admiring her small, firm, denim-clad rear end and those long legs as she walked into the living room to gather up her things. I waited until she was out the front door and onto the porch before I followed her. As I locked up, I told myself sternly that this was my *client*, for God's sake. Professionalism, Reece. Right.

* * * * *

I drove Tonia to pick up her car from the University parking lot, and followed her home. It was fully dark, and would soon rain, I realized. Wonderful. The evening was shaping up to be truly enjoyable.

I pulled my MG into Tonia's driveway behind her chocolate Honda Accord and hurried up the walk. She was waiting for me at the front door of the condominium. As she closed the door behind me, there was a moment of awkwardness in the hall. I groaned mentally. Would I have to start that "Jabberwocky" stuff again?

"Caitlin," she said reasonably, turning to face me. In the cramped space we were maybe two feet apart. I was suddenly aware of her scent—equal parts shampoo, leather jacket and Tonia. "Why—"

I told myself her question was a professional inquiry, and tried to control my breathing. "Why do I need to come with you tonight? Simple. Because I've got a bad feeling," I told her truthfully. "Something about this just isn't right. I don't know what it is yet, but I will. And I don't think you should be left alone to play target." That had come out rather well, I though. My voice had never even quavered.

She blinked several times, then turned to go upstairs. "Go on in," she told me. I made sure the front door deadbolt was turned, and went into the living room. "I've got to hurry," she called from the stairs. "You know where everything is from the other night, I expect. Just help yourself."

I found a beer in the fridge and slumped on the sofa, feigning a pose of nonchalance: Caitlin Reece, cool, tough private eye. Always in control. Yup. I snorted, and swallowed the entire beer, recalling hopefully the devastating effect alcohol always had on my libido. I prayed for speedy results. Having another beer seemed like a very good idea, so I did. Then, thinking I'd rest for just a few minutes, I closed my eyes.

"Caitlin," someone said softly. A hand shook me awake.

Tonia. I came awake with a start. "Mmmph," I muttered. "Sorry. Must be my decongestant." She was sitting on the back of the sofa, her hand on my shoulder. I prayed for strength and rose to my feet. Taking a step, I turned and checked to see that the sofa was indeed between us.

She looked terrific. Her hair was freshly brushed and shiny, and she had traded her green sweater and jeans for a pair of grey flannel pants and a blue turtleneck sweater that exactly matched her eyes. She gave me that unreadable look again, then smiled quickly. I was glad the couch was where it was. "I know you think you have to come tonight," she said, "so I won't try to talk you out of it, but surely you don't want to wait in the car."

"It's not an especially appealing prospect," I agreed.

"I thought not," she said. "So I've got a better idea."

"Oh?" I inquired, hoping she couldn't read my mind. I, too, had a better idea.

72

"Yes. I've called Kay and told her that a friend dropped in unexpectedly. She doesn't mind. Setting another place for dinner would be easy, she said." She smiled mysteriously at me. "But you might mind."

I had not intentions of attending this little soirée, dressed as I was in half of Smythe's Metro Gas uniform, but wondered why Tonia thought I might mind. Did she imagine me to be so keenly aware of my low social station that I would be embarrassed to mingle with the upper crust? Did she believe that we thugs couldn't tell one fork from another? That we would drink from the finger bowl? "Why might I mind?" I asked.

Her eyes sparkled mischief. "I hardly think you'd feel at home with three lesbian separatists, a proponent of nonviolence, and a rather radical lesbian author."

"What, no partridge in a pear tree?" I inquired sarcastically.

Tonia actually grinned, and I decided the wisest course of action was to refuse to rise to her bait. Did she really imagine, now that I knew the guest list, that I'd want to attend and trade pithy remarks with her dinner party companions? Perhaps she planned to sit back and snicker as I did verbal battle. Well, I'm afraid I have very little tolerance for philosophic discussions. It has always seemed so much easier to just *do* something instead of talking a subject to death. A sudden image of myself doffing my .357 Magnum and putting it on the dining room sideboard came abruptly into my mind, and I chuckled. *That* might produce a round of lively conversation. No, Caitlin, I told myself. Be good.

"I think I'll pass," I informed Tonia. "But thanks for the thought, anyhow."

She grinned again, and I realized suddenly that she had taken a great deal of pleasure in setting me up for this. I felt confused. What was going on here?

"Well, perhaps you'll come in for coffee and dessert when you get back from the studio," she said meekly.

"Mmmm," I said enigmatically. "We'll see."

* * * * *

"You're sure you won't change your mind?" Tonia asked as I dropped her at the address she gave me—a little house across from the beach on Dallas Road.

"Maybe later," I told her. "For coffee and dessert." And a little wringing of Tonia Konig's neck.

She smiled at me, and I realized that wringing was not what I had in mind for this particular neck. Fortunately, she got out of the car at that moment and walked toward the house, thus sparing me the effort of further poetic recitations. Those efforts were getting tedious, and I have never been noted for my iron self-control. Besides, something was happening here. Just what I wasn't sure. I groaned a little as I backed the MG out of the driveway. Professionalism, Caitlin, I reminded myself. Next thing you know, you'll be pawing the turf. Right, I agreed again. Professionalism.

With difficulty, I wrenched my thoughts from Tonia to Val. That was good for a massive infusion of guilt. Val and Tonia were lovers; Val was my paying client. What are you thinking about, you dumb broad, I asked myself irritably. I pointed the MG toward Beacon Hill Park and drove along by the dark sea, brooding, my burgeoning concupiscence neatly nipped in its steamy bud.

Chapter 7

The television newsroom was a scene of controlled chaos. It was almost airtime and harried young men and women were scurrying back and forth to and from the control room with videotape cassettes and sheaves of paper. Valerie and her co-anchor — a pleasant looking redhead named Guy McLeod — sat in their places at the newsroom set, having their makeup applied by a willowy young man in a cerise shirt.

"Can I help you?" a pleasant female voice behind me asked.

I turned around. She looked to be about seventeen, with a short blonde crewcut on top, and longer hair in back. Conservative punk. I looked more closely. Nope, the back was definitely orange. I amended my opinion about conservative.

"I'm Mimi Angstrom, script assistant," she told me, showing about a pound of aluminum braces on her teeth. My God, she looked young.

"Val invited me to watch," I said, fibbing a little. "I don't know where to sit."

"Oh," Mimi said in surprise. "This is really Val's day to have guests, isn't it?"

My stomach tightened a little. "Is it?"

"Yeah. Know that man over there?"

I looked where she was pointing. Off to one side, out of everyone's way, a prosperous looking, beefy man sat in a canvas chair well behind the cameras.

"No, who is he?"

"Baxter Buchanan," she said somewhat sarcastically, apparently emboldened by the fact that I was not a close friend of the Buchanan family. "He of the shiny black Jaguar. Do you know his license plates say WINNER?"

I stored this bit of information away for future use. "Does he drop in like this often?"

She nodded. "Just to keep Val on her toes, I guess. He's pretty jealous." She found me a chair, and I sat against the back wall. Mimi perched on an enormous roll of cable and scowled at Buchanan.

I decided to see what other bits of information she might be willing to divulge. "Jealousy," I sighed, arching my eyebrows meaningfully. "That kind of thing can be a real drag. Poor Val."

She nodded her head vigorously, glad to have found an ally. "He may be an MLA and all, but he's a real turd," she said, not bothering to lower her voice. I guessed she had tangled with old Winner more than once.

"Mmm," I agreed. "Val deserves better."

"You bet she does! That pudgy little creep thinks he owns her. He only drops in like this to see if he can catch her screwing the sound man. Or the makeup boy." She looked up to see someone waving frantically at her. "Oops. Gotta go." She launched herself off the cable.

"The always anonymous beast," I said without thinking.

"What?"

"Oh, sorry. That's a line from a poem. The husband has an overactive imagination and sees potential adulterers everywhere. But his wife is really innocent—there is no adulterer—and so the always anonymous beast is the husband's jealousy. Sort of like Baxter and Val."

"I like it," she said. "Beastly Baxter Buchanan. But you know, Val's never given him any reason to act the way he does. Even if she did have the hots for someone else—and who could blame her—she'd never sneak around like he thinks she does. The lady has too much class. Listen, I really hafta run." She trotted across the studio, leaving me to my solitary contemplation of the uxorious Baxter.

So he was jealous, was he? Well, Val had told me as much. But whereas his suspicions had previously been groundless, now things were different. At least I presumed they were. Val and Tonia hadn't seemed especially warm towards each other when I had seen them together last night, but they had been lovers at one time. Or had they? What did the letters really say, anyhow? I realized I didn't know. How much did Val have to be truly guilty about? For all I knew, the two of them may have just held hands and looked soulfully into each other's orbs. If so, that would have been Val's style, I guessed. Somehow, Tonia didn't seem the sort to put up with that kind of self-denying nonsense. Well, that would account for the awkward atmosphere around them. I decided I needed to know what *was* going on. Or had gone on.

I recalled Val's guilty, furtive fear, and Tonia's go-to-hell outrage. Two very different reactions to the prospect of being found out. Was it possible that Val, having discovered at her age a *grande passion* for another woman, had suddenly gotten cold feet? Perhaps she had decided she wanted out of the relationship before it had even gotten well started. I could understand that. The jump from heterosexuality to lesbianism entails a lot more than a leap into a different bed—it's a leap into a different world. Maybe Val couldn't cope. She seemed to have an excessively developed sense of what other people might think. In my experience, people are so fickle that even the juiciest scandal has a life of somewhat less than a week. But perhaps Val couldn't stand living through that week. Or the changes that would come after. She would need an incredibly thick skin, a pretty well-integrated personality, and a lot of guts. Val seemed to me a little light in the guts department.

So maybe Val had looked at the ramifications of loving another woman, and had been scared to death. So scared that she'd run for the hills? I was willing to bet on it. I liked the theory. It explained a lot. Even the Dark Lady sonnet Tonia had asked me about, which I guessed hadn't been an idle question.

Well, I couldn't sit here all night. Obviously, Val hadn't met with any skaters. She seemed okay. And with hubby hovering near, what harm could possibly befall her?

I got up and walked across the set. Val saw me coming and smiled a little crookedly. Guy McLeod shuffled his papers and made no effort to give us any privacy. He gave Val a sidelong look of resentment, and I smiled at what I saw. Oho, I thought. Playing second fiddle doesn't agree with the young Mr. McLeod. Never mind that Val had been in this business fifteen years longer than he had. He resented her nonetheless.

"Hello, Val," I said neutrally, bearing in mind McLeod's vibrating antennae. "Can I call you at home later?" I asked her. "I have some interesting information for you on that project we were discussing the other night. We should talk about it."

She closed her eyes briefly, and I could see by what massive effort of will she was keeping herself under control.

"I've been expecting to hear from you," she told me cryptically. "But I may be tied up for a few days. I'm not sure. If I'm not, I'd like to get together with you." She looked directly at me, and her composure slipped, just a little. She was a desperately frightened woman, I realized. I wondered if the presence of the possessive Buchanan had anything to do with her state of mind. Probably.

"No problem," I said reassuringly. "I'll be sort of tied up, too, but I can make time for you."

"Thanks, Caitlin," she said. "I'll call you as soon as I can."

I winked at her. Chin up, kid. She smiled weakly back. McLeod rustled his papers and looked smug. On the way across the set I took a little detour. I wanted a closer look at Baxter Buchanan.

I circled around to one side, stepping over cables and dodging cameras, and arranged to pass in front of him.

"Excuse me," I said, forcing a smile as I momentarily blocked his view of Valerie. He blinked, seeming to come back to earth from some distant plane, and turned to me, his expression quite blank. At that moment Val laughed, and like a dog attuned to his master's voice, Baxter swivelled back toward the set. And I saw something I was clearly not meant to see—the coals of a well banked range smoldering somewhere behind his eyes. But there was something else, too. Something quiet and gleeful and deadly. I stopped dead in my tracks. Where had I seen something like that before? Suddenly it came to me, and I felt as if some entity had touched the back of my neck with bared teeth. Marc Bergeron had looked like that. Buchanan turned to me slowly, and I saw the mask of normalcy fall back into place. The MLA from Okanagan South looked up and smiled.

"No problem," he said. I had already forgotten what action of mine he was responding to.

I muttered something, and walked toward the door. Chilled to my bones, I made my way out to the MG, and locked myself in.

* * * * *

As I drove back to Dallas Road, I made a mental note to find out whatever I could about Buchanan. Maybe he was just weird. Your standard overly possessive husband. But I was willing to believe what I had seen. A hunch? The Llewelyn prescience? Whichever. After a few minutes my flesh stopped crawling, and my stomach began to rumble. Real life asserting itself again. Coffee and dessert just wouldn't do it, I decided, and pulled into McDonald's with guilty thoughts of Yvonne. However, I managed to devour a Big Mac, large fries, and a chocolate milkshake without a twinge of regret. I think McDonald's adds something to their food. Something that undermines all our good intentions. Something addicting. Ah well. I licked the last of the sauce off my fingers and sighed. Time for coffee, dessert, and the tail end of a rousing philosophic discussion. Oh goody.

* * * * *

"Come on in," a slim, grey-haired woman said, meeting me at the door. "Tonia told us you were coming. I'm Kay Allen."

"Caitlin Reece," I said, stepping in gratefully out of the rain. Kay, an attractive fifty-year-old in black pants and heavy white fisherman's knit sweater, locked the door behind me.

"Everyone's downstairs watching the movie," she said.

For one long moment I wondered if I was at the right house. What movie? I must have looked as uncertain as I felt, because she laughed a little and ushered me into the kitchen. A pot of coffee was just finishing its perk cycle, and like a good Pavlovian subject, I began to salivate. She checked on something in the oven, and a wonderful odor of cinnamon escaped. I suddenly decided I didn't care if I was at the wrong house. I'd bluff.

"Make yourself comfortable," she said, and I took a seat at the big pine table in the corner. "Coffee?"

I nodded. "With milk, please."

She smiled and handed me a big white ceramic mug with a cobalt whale on it. The coffee smelled delicious. "There's someone here who'd like to talk to you," she said, looking me over with frank interest.

"Oh?" I couldn't imagine who.

"Yes. Jan Principal. It's her movie we're watching. Lorimar bought one of her books."

I paused, the coffee mug halfway to my lips. "Jan?" I couldn't believe it. The last time I had seen Jan had been . . . how long *had* it been? I closed my eyes. Texada Island. Four years ago this month. I sighed.

"Jan told us what you did for Lorraine Shaver."

I raised my eyebrows. Jan's friend Lorraine had been my first client. Lorraine's husband had kidnapped their three-year-old daughter. Lorraine had been half out of her mind with worry because the husband was an abusive, alcoholic bully from whom Lorraine had fled eleven months earlier. She was unwilling to go through the courts to get the child back because the husband threatened to expose her lesbian lifestyle. It was a no-win situation. Jan came to see me to ask for my legal opinion. After I explained that I was no longer working in the Crown Prosecutor's office, I gave my legal opinion, and dispensed some free layperson's advice, too—stay out of the courts, and send someone reliable to get the child back. Lorraine offered me the job. Once I satisfied myself that the child really *would* be better off with her, I took it.

I made an equivocal noise.

"Are you doing the same sort of thing for Tonia?" she asked, pale eyes sparkling with interest.

"What did Tonia say?" I countered.

Kay made a small moue of disappointment. "Only that you were . . . friends."

Friends? Ye gods. "Well . . . "

"Well what? Caitlin Reece, at a loss for words?"

"Jan!" I exclaimed.

Kay disappeared into the lower part of the house, and Jan closed the door after her. She stood against it, looking at me. She hadn't changed a bit. Tonight she was dressed in a black wool sweater, black pants, and boots. Her blonde hair had been recently cut in the long-layered shag that suited her so well. She looked like an Amazon, and I couldn't help grinning.

"Four years," she said. "You know, I've been keeping myself informed about your exploits. Some of them have been pretty wild. Not bad, for someone who had retired from the human race at thirty-five," she teased.

"It's all your fault," I told her. "If you hadn't come to hassle me that day, I might still be fishing. Have you learned how to swim yet?" I teased back.

She shook her head. "Hell, no. I'm waiting for another smelly young ex-CP lawyer to come along and tackle me."

We laughed, and I thought how good it was to see her. I wished Texada Island closer, and myself less busy.

"I'm glad you're all right," she said.

"I really am," I told her. "Thank you."

"Good," she said and we smiled at each other. "Pack a toothbrush and come over some weekend."

"I'll try," I said. "I'd like that."

The door opened behind Jan, and Tonia emerged. She looked from Jan to me curiously.

"Ready to go?" I asked her.

She nodded. "I'll just get my coat."

"Good luck," Jan said, putting an arm around my shoulder and hugging me. "I mean that. Tonia's a good person. I hope you can help her."

"I'm doing my best," I said. "But so far that hasn't been good enough." I put my hands in my pockets and fiddled with my car keys. A sudden thought occurred to me. "Listen, Jan," I said, lowering my voice. "I might want to talk to you. About Tonia. Are you going back to Texada tonight?"

She shook her head. "I'm staying with Kay for a few days. Then I'm flying to Toronto. If you want to talk, it will have be before Friday."

* * * * *

I had no wish to talk about Jan Principal, so I steered Tonia in another direction before she could ask any questions.

"Does Baxter Buchanan know you?" I asked Tonia as we pulled out of the driveway of Kay's house and onto Dallas Road.

"I don't think so," she said. "Oh, I suppose he might have seen me on a talk show, or on the interview Val did with me. But it's unlikely. I've never been to the apartment when he's there. Which is seldom. He spends most of his time at the family farm in the Okanagan Valley, on the mainland."

"Lucky Val," I said, recalling the way I had shivered when Baxter dismissed me. To my surprise, Tonia spoke my thoughts aloud.

"If she doesn't get away from him, he'll do something really crazy," she said feelingly. "He knows he can't have her, but he doesn't want to give her up to anyone else."

The dog in the manger syndrome. And from what I had seen of Baxter, he wasn't about to let anyone else even close to the manger.

I decided to ask the questions that had been bothering me about Tonia's and Val's relationship. What the hell—Tonia could only tell me to mind my own business. "Is Val leaving Baxter for you?"

Tonia burst out laughing. "God, no! Sorry, Caitlin. No, it's not like that. I'm very fond of Val, but I have no illusions that we could ever have had anything together. At one time we both thought it was possible, but maybe that was mostly wishful thinking. You see, Val's suffering from a severe case of the guilts. She may or may not get over them." She laughed again, a little bitterly. "The irony of it is that we haven't *done* anything for her to feel guilty about. I think her attraction to me has simply served as a focus for a lot of guilt she's been carrying around."

"Guilt about what?"

Tonia shrugged. "About not being a successful wife. About not wanting to have children. About not wanting a life in her husband's shadow. About loathing politics. About being more successful at her work than Baxter is at his. About being attracted to women." She added the last point very softly: "About thinking she was in love with me."

"Hmm," I replied. "That's an awful lot of guilt." I thought over what Tonia had said, and concluded that their relationship had never had a chance.

"Now what?" I asked her. "For you and Val."

"First we sort out this blackmail mess. Then, if Val is still in one piece, we have to . . . conclude. Wrap it up. Maybe we can still be friends. Maybe not."

"Hmm," I said again. So I had been right in my sensing something of the sort when I had seen them together. Well, first things first. Sorting out this blackmail mess, as Tonia put it. That, at least, was something I could understand.

"Are you surprised?" Tonia said, breaking into my thoughts.

It was my turn to laugh. "At what?"

"At my cold and heartless analysis of the situation."

"Hardly."

84

"Damn it, Caitlin, you're impenetrable," Tonia said in exasperation.

"No, I'm not," I said, tiring of the image she seemed determined to create of me. Tough little thug. "You just haven't found the chinks yet."

That must have given her something to think about, because she was quiet all the way to Foul Bay Road. Which was just as well, because I was dead tired. Further conversation was impossible. My brain, along with my body, was limp with fatigue. I needed sleep, not banter.

"I'll call you tomorrow," I told Tonia as we pulled into the Uplands condominiums.

She nodded, and started to get out. "That's fine with me." One hand on the car door, she turned back to me. "Thanks," she said.

"For what?"

"Just . . . thanks." She got out quickly, closed the door, and hurried through the rain up to her front porch. In a moment she was inside, and I saw lights go on. I backed the MG out of the driveway and started for home.

To Tonia's credit, she hadn't asked one question about Jan. Nor had she baited me again about the dinner party guests. Did we have a truce? I yawned until my jaws cracked. Stranger things had happened.

WEDNESDAY

Chapter 8

The morning dawned improbably bright and sunny. Coy April. Making us believe in life again. I staggered out of bed and stood at the window, bemused. Outside, the apple tree's resident robins were busy setting up housekeeping amid the pink blossoms. Maybe they knew something I didn't. I permitted myself a tiny surge of optimism.

Dressing quickly, I followed the glorious smell of coffee to the kitchen. The electronic brain of my automatic Krups coffee maker had done it again. Such a faithful minion—never a complaint, always with the coffee ready on time. And it didn't chatter to me as I read the morning paper. Why, I thought guiltily, it was better than a wife. Caitlin, old kid, you're pretty far gone down the road to misanthropy when you prefer the company of your Krups to that of another human being. The phone rang at just that instant, ending further thoughts of electronic companionship.

"Caitlin?" It was Tonia. She sounded madder than hell.

"Yes?"

"Why are you having my house watched?"

"I'm not."

"Well, someone is."

A little spider of fear walked across my neck. "Where are you now?"

"At school."

"Okay. Why don't you meet me at your house. Give me about twenty minutes. And just to be on the safe side, don't get out of your car until you see me."

Silence. "All right," she said finally.

I hung up and thoughtfully finished the rest of my coffee.

* * * * *

I drove down Oak Bay Avenue to Beach Drive just to get a glimpse of the ocean. Today it was worth it. As I passed the park in front of Willows Beach, I could see the water sparkling through the trees, and a few brave boats scudding along in the straits, kicking up rooster tails of foam. There really isn't a name for the color of northern seas under a spring sky. Pity. The Inuit people have several hundred adjectives to qualify the word snow. So what's the matter with us? Dull-souled Anglo Saxons that we are, we can put people on the moon, but are defeated by description. Must technology preclude poetry? I sighed and turned inland into Uplands.

If Vancouver is the San Francisco of Canada, and Victoria the Santa Barbara, then Uplands is the Palm Springs. There are probably more millionaires per acre in Uplands than anywhere else in the country. Of course it looks nothing at all like Palm Springs, but it has a similar aura. A hush of wealth. It always reminds me of an enormous private park, with its huge Gary Oaks, lush rhododendrons, immaculately tended lawns, and here and there, tucked away at the end of winding drives, or discreetly hidden behind stone walls, the modest mansions of the ultra rich. Life at the top in Victoria.

I pulled into Tonia's development—the new townhouses that some canny speculator had built just on the fringe of Uplands. I realized I had never been here in daylight, and was disappointed to note that they looked even more unprepossessing by day. The houses in the crowded enclave were joined together at strange angles, making the development look as if the contractor's three-year-old had had a hand in its planning. Too bad. With a little more foresight, a really attractive development might have resulted. I simply couldn't imagine living there.

I pulled into the driveway, and Tonia's car pulled in after mine. She ran up the steps and into the house, and I followed.

"He was right out there," she told me, taking me into the dining room and pulling back the curtain. "Just at the corner of the fence, where my property ends."

I opened the sliding glass doors and went across the back yard. Where Tonia's stained wooden fence ended and a hedge of cedars began was a small gap a person might squeeze through if he were slim, but it wasn't a short cut that led anywhere. Except to Tonia's back yard. A dozen cigarette butts were ground into the damp earth. Tonia was right—someone had been here, just standing and smoking. And there was nothing to look at but Tonia's house.

I went back inside and locked the sliding door. Then I went on into the kitchen. There was something else I wanted to see. I stood in the kitchen, looking out over the cedar fence to the tall pines that grew thick on the University grounds just across Landsdowne Road. It was a perfect line of sight. Maybe a hundred feet. Not far at all. The photographer must have stationed himself within those trees, and taken pictures. For the burglary? Or the blackmail? I shook my head. Maybe when I got the photos back there would be some answers. I closed the shutters, blocking the view of the kitchen, and went up to find Tonia.

On impulse, I went into the spare room—Tonia's study—to take another look at the pines across the road. I stood in the middle of the room, looking pensively out to the trees. Thinking I saw something, I took one step forward, and there was, almost simultaneously a sharp *crack*, a shattering of glass, and a bright, hot agony in my left shoulder. I fell to the floor, too surprised to yell.

"What's happening?" Tonia called, coming at a dead run.

I ground my teeth against the pain. "Get down on the floor!" She stood there staring, and I kicked out at her with one sneakered foot. "*Get down*! Someone's shooting at us!"

She threw herself to the rug and crawled toward me.

I turned over and looked at the window. From my vantage point I could see only sky. No pine trees. Good. That meant the sniper couldn't see us, either. I rolled on my side and drew my gun.

"Caitlin, be careful!" she whispered.

I scrambled over to the window and cautiously raised my head above the sill. Nothing happened. I brought my gun up, braced it on the sill, and sighted down the barrel. There was nothing but pine tree. The sniper was gone. Agile little bastard. I slumped to the floor.

"Now what?" Tonia asked.

"Now we stay here until I figure out whether or not I can crawl to the bathroom. Or wherever you keep your first aid supplies."

I put my gun down and risked a look at my arm. It could have been worse. The bullet had ploughed through my navy windbreaker and wool turtleneck, leaving a ragged rip. I parted the fabric and looked inside. There was a long, deep gash in my shoulder muscle, sullenly seeping blood. I decided I didn't want to look at it any more and lay down on the rug.

"Caitlin!" Tonia exclaimed, finally realizing what I'd been looking at. "You've been shot!" She sat up.

I lurched over and pushed her down with my good arm. "Stay down, okay? I'm not entirely sure he's gone. Let's not give him another target."

Tonia wriggled around until she was on my left side, leaning over me. She touched the bloody rip in my jacket. "Why, Caitlin?" she asked me. "I can't understand why this is happening!"

"Neither can I," I told her, "but you can be damned sure I'm going to find out." Several minutes had now passed, and my arm was beginning to hurt like hell. "Let's crawl on into the hall," I suggested. "I'll go first. You shut this door behind us."

Tonia slammed the door, and we crouched side by side, looking at each other in the gloom of the hallway. Her eyes were enormous. I ground my teeth. There's nothing like getting shot to banish lustful thoughts. You're safe today, Konig, I thought. From me, at least.

I heaved myself to my feet and wobbled into the bathroom, shedding jacket and sweater as I went. I turned on the light and looked at the damage in the mirror. And immediately regretted it. I always did hate the sight of blood. Especially my own.

"Shit," I said weakly and sat down on the closed lid of the toilet.

Tonia was busy hauling things out of the medicine cabinet. "I don't know what to do," she said in a panic. "It looks awful. It probably needs suturing. Let me call—"

"No. Don't call anyone. You wanted to keep the police out of this, didn't you?"

She nodded, comprehension dawning.

"Do you have some peroxide?"

"Yes."

"Give it to me." I opened the bottle, took a deep breath and poured the peroxide onto my gashed arm. For a moment, nothing happened. Then the pain hit. Tonia caught me as I oozed onto the floor. Somewhere far away I heard the bottle break. I could only have been out for a few minutes, and when I came around I was lying on something incredibly soft, something that smelled good. I opened my eyes. I was lying on Tonia's navy lambskin jacket. She had rolled it up and put it under my head. I looked up. She was just finishing putting a patch on my arm. "Mmmph," I managed.

"Thank God you're all right," Tonia said.

Well, that was debatable. But I sat up anyhow. Acting like a wimp is bad for client morale. In a few minutes I figured I'd be able to stand. Terrific progress was being made here. "Yeah, I'm all right. Getting shot tends to slow me down a little, that's all."

Tonia was horrified. "You mean this has happened to you before?"

"Once," I confessed. "When I was doing something about as dumb as making a target of myself in your study window."

"I thought you just . . . solved mysteries. Helped people."

I smiled ruefully. "Well, sometimes I have to take a few lumps along the way."

I decided I didn't want to put my bloodstained sweater back on, and asked Tonia for something to wear. While she was gone I decided to stand up. We couldn't sit here chatting on the bathroom floor all day. I lurched to my feet and grabbed hold of the basin. When I didn't fall over I celebrated by washing my face and cleaning the dried blood off my arm.

Tonia reappeared with a burgundy sweatshirt, and slipped it over my head. "Nice color," I commented. "At least if I leak, the blood won't show."

I decided to do something really difficult, and took a few steps. My feet seemed to be working fine, but I suspected it was only temporary. "How long will it take you to pack a bag?" I asked Tonia.

She looked at me, eyes wide, and swallowed audibly. "About five minutes."

"Good," I told her. "I'll just lean against the wall here while you do it. And don't forget any books or papers you might need."

"Where am I going?" Tonia asked.

"My place. Uplands Estates is clearly a very unhealthy place to live."

"But it was you they were after, not me."

I glared at her, and she backed down, evidently thinking it best to humor me. "Still, better safe than sorry," I told her. "And hurry up, please."

She disappeared into the bedroom, emerging a few minutes later with a small suitcase. "I need a manuscript from my study," she told me. "I have to deliver a talk on Sunday."

I nodded. "Get it. It's safe." I had begun to feel terrible, and wondered how I was going to make it down the stairs to my car.

"I'll put this load in your car," Tonia said. "Then put my car in the garage. I'll put the lights on a timer." She looked at me apprehensively. "Are you sure you're all right?"

"No to both parts of that question."

She hurried away, and I closed my eyes. I wanted nothing more than to slither down the wall, lay my head on that thick blue carpet, and crawl away someplace where there was no pain.

"Caitlin," Tonia said, "I'm back. Let me help." She put my good arm over her shoulder and took my weight as we carefully descended the stairs. What a waste, I thought, as her warm hand clasped my bare skin under the sweatshirt. She deposited me in the passenger seat of my MG and then backed the car out of the driveway. I had the presence of mind to tell her where to take me before I passed out.

*****

Tonia brought me to an old and very special friend, Maggie Kent. In 1956 she'd had her license pulled for performing an abortion on a thirteen-year-old raped by her own father. Since then, she'd been practicing underground medicine, barely scraping out a living. I wouldn't have dreamed of letting anyone but Maggie take care of my ailments. We kept each other's secrets.

Numbed, sutured, and chemically calmed, I then allowed Tonia to put me back in the passenger seat and drive us home. All I could think about was going down for the count when I crossed my threshold. That, and the clock ticking down to Saturday.

As we turned onto Oak Bay Avenue, it started to rain. So much for the promise of a glorious day. April had fooled us again. And, for a variety of reasons, I felt like the biggest fool of all.

"I need your help," I said, as we pulled into the driveway. "Doc Kent's chemicals are about to do me in, and I can't afford to mess up any more." She looked at me curiously. "I'll take it off your half of the bill," I told her, giggling a little. God, what had Maggie pumped into me?

Once we'd locked ourselves safely in my living room, I leaned against the bookcase to deliver my swan song.

"What I want you to do is to call Val for me. Make sure she's all right."

Tonia looked at me curiously. "Why shouldn't she be?"

I weaved towards my bedroom. "Just do it," I called. This was no time to discuss with Tonia my suspicion that the bullet that had creased my shoulder had not been meant for me at all.

"Caitlin!" I heard her say in alarm. Then I heard nothing else.

* * * * *

I opened my eyes and had an attack of déjà vu. Where am I, I yammered to my brain. Texada, it suggested. There was a woman sitting in a chair by my bed, reading. The lamplight shone on her glossy hair. I knew her, but the name just wouldn't come. I closed my eyes, waiting for it all to make sense. No, it was unlikely that this was Texada, because Jan's hair was blonde, not black. I squinted. Whoever this was, our faces were on the same level, and I looked at her from my horizontal position, wondering if this was some steamy romantic dream. If so, it was a pretty dull one. Surely my id could do better. If this wasn't Jan, just who was it? I closed my eyes, then opened them again.

Tonia looked at me over the magazine she was reading—a current copy of *The Canadian Forum*. Boy, what excitement. I couldn't wait to see what happened next. Maybe she'd read to me. Some pithy political commentary—the stuff fantasies are made of.

"Caitlin," she said in relief, putting the magazine down. "How are you feeling?"

Nope, this was no fantasy—everyone felt terrific in romantic dreams. This must be real life. Too bad. "I feel awful," I told her. "What are you doing here, anyhow? Watching me snore can't be much fun."

"You scared me to death. I called your doctor friend, Maggie Kent."

"Why?" I inquired gruffly. "You're not my nurse."

"No," she said, putting a hand on my forehead, "I'm not."

Real life or fantasy, I decided this was a dumb conversation. What I really wanted was to be left alone so I could have a good cry. My arm hurt like hell, the hours were slipping away, and I was feeling very sorry for myself.

She got up from her chair, poured some water, and brought it to me with a small capsule.

97

"What's this?" I asked. "Unless it's hemlock, I don't want it."

"Doctor Kent said to take it. It'll help the pain. And make you sleep."

I was tempted. An extend period of oblivion seemed very attractive. "What time is it?"

"Almost midnight."

"Of what day?"

"Wednesday."

Thank God it was still the same day. Well, maybe I would take the pill. "Will I be able to get up in the morning?" I asked Tonia. "This won't turn me into a zombie or anything, will it?"

"I don't think so. But what if it did?"

"I have work to do," I said. "People are counting on me. As Frost said, 'But I have promises to keep, and miles to go before I sleep.' Of course, I don't have miles to go *tonight*, but—"

"Shut up and take the damned pill," Tonia said roughly. "You'll be up at the crack of dawn ready to slay dragons or whatever you think you need to do. God, Caitlin, give yourself a break."

I shook my head but took the pill. "I'm hold you responsible," I told her. "Did you call Val?"

"Yes. She's fine. Enjoying a domestic evening with Baxter."

"Sounds thrilling," I said. I began to count the seconds, waiting for the pain in my arm to stop. God, when? It throbbed with every one of my heartbeats, a slow, dark, persistent pulsing of agony. "What about you?" I whispered, closing my eyes. "It's past everyone's bedtime. Why don't you just toddle off to the spare bedroom? I'm okay now."

"I'll go in a few minutes," she said. "Do you want anything?"

Between the pain killer and my own fatigue, I was having trouble concentrating. "Just some more water," I told her.

She held a glass to my lips and I drank what I could. She settled down again in her armchair, and switched off the bedside lamp.

The pain killer was making me giddy, and I hung onto the mattress, fearing I might float off. I felt light and insubstantial, and imagined my spirit to be a bird, beating its wings in preparation to take flight from my body. The wings beat in rhythm with my pain, and I began to be afraid that when those wings of agony stopped beating, my spirit would leave my body behind, a useless shell from which it had finally fled. But before the wings stopped, a black tidal wave rolled over me, and I rose to greet it, my mind appalled at the eagerness with which I embraced oblivion.

* * * * *

Just before dawn, I awakened. I was lying on my right side, knees bent. Someone lay behind me, one arm around my waist. Her hand clasped mine, and I could feel warm breath on the back of my neck. I groaned, and in the crepuscular gloom, closed my eyes and wept.

THURSDAY

Chapter 9

When my alarm went off at eight-thirty, I briefly considered hurling it through the window. Without thinking I rolled over on my left arm, and cursed unimaginatively as it reminded me that I had been shot only yesterday. Then I remembered. Tonia. I sat on the edge of the bed, wondering what had prompted her to do what she did. She *had* been in my bed when I had awakened early this morning, hadn't she? That certainly hadn't been Repo's arm around me. However, I was definitely alone now.

I got up, and on my way to the bathroom, passed the door of the spare bedroom. It was firmly closed. I raised my hand to knock, then decided against it. I didn't have time for this right now. Hell, I didn't even understand the mystery I had been hired to solve—did I want to take on another one, too?

I showered as best I could, combed my hair, and dressed, making enough noise to wake the dead, but Tonia didn't emerge. I left some food for Repo who was, I supposed, snoozing away with Tonia, took one last look at the closed door, and left the house. Later, I decided. I had business to attend to.

* * * * *

The Oak Bay Police Department is a little Tudor cottage marooned on a macadam beach. Clearly, no Canadian Canute had been able to hold back the asphalt waves lapping its door. For years it handled complaints no more serious than nocturnally yapping dogs and misplaced rose shears. For the inhabitants of Oak Bay, the only indication that the force was with us was the punctilious policing of on-street parking in Oak Bay Village—a high-crime district if there ever was one. Woe betide the driver unable to puzzle out the meaning of the splashes of curbside color that governed parking times: white for one hour, green for half an hour, yellow for fifteen minutes, and red for pickup/dropoff. What's hard about that? Even today, constables customarily lurk behind lampposts, rubbing their hands in glee, waiting eagerly to slap tickets on Porsches from Pittsburgh or Lincolns from Los Angeles which linger too long in the yellow zone.

Gary Alexander, aka Sandy, was not a constable. He did not write parking tickets. He was a detective in the Major Crimes Division, which, sad to say, no longer included barking dogs or lost property. Like an apple rotting from within, the world was going to hell, and the rot had finally erupted even here in peaceful Oak Bay.

I liked Sandy. He was a direct, no-nonsense Scot, about fifty-five, with a ferociously bristling moustache, and an unshakably sunny outlook on life. I'd had occasion to work

104

with him when I was in the CP's office, and we always got on well together. He was one of the few men I knew who didn't feel that my sexual orientation was a lamentable condition to be cured by a night of male attention. Actually, I don't know what he thought as we'd never discussed the subject. It had come up once, years ago, and he hadn't turned a hair. I was glad. Sandy was a damned good detective, a very useful contact, and a good friend. Today I had come to call in a marker.

He met me outside the police station. "Let's not talk here. I'll buy you coffee," he suggested.

We drove to The Blethering Place, a tea room in the Village, and found a place to park. In the green zone, I noted. The place was busy, even at ten a.m., but we managed to find a table by the window. I ordered a cheese scone and coffee Sandy only tea. After the waitress brought our order, he pulled a sheaf of papers from the inside pocket of his tweed jacket and scowled at me.

"What are you meddling around with now, Caitlin?"

"Why? Did those serial numbers I gave you short circuit your computer?"

"Not our computer. Metro Victoria's. They've had a rash of burglaries since last fall and no leads. Mostly electronic gear. But it hasn't been fenced yet. Or if it has, it's been taken off the island."

"Hmmm," I said thoughtfully. That the case belong to Metro made me feel better, because I would have hated to hold back on Sandy. But I had no intentions of surrendering the boy burglars just yet. No sirree. "May I see the list?"

Sandy's moustache quivered with anticipation. "Why? What do you know?"

I held out my hand. He sighed and handed over the list. "I'd like to keep this," I told him.

He shook his head helplessly. "All right. Do you know what you're doing?"

I shrugged. "The day before yesterday I hadn't a clue. Yesterday I began to see a glimmer of hope. Today, the glimmer is a gleam."

"I should know better than to ask," he said. He looked at his watch. "Is that all? If you want any more information today I'll have to go and tickle yon wee electronic beastie some more. But I'll be in court all afternoon, so I couldn't do it until tomorrow."

"I think this will be good enough," I said. "I appreciate it. Thanks a lot, Sandy."

He looked at me for a long moment, and sighed. "I shouldn't let you have that list. And whatever's going on, it's probably something you shouldn't get mixed up in. I suppose there's no point in asking you to leave it alone?"

I shook my head.

"I thought not, but I owe you." He smiled and stood up, leaving a handful of change on the table. As if in afterthought, he asked, "You wouldn't want to drop around and have dinner with Mary and me, would you?" He peered at me closely. "You're looking a wee bit gaunt."

I laughed. "I'd love to come for dinner. Does Mary still make haggis?"

He swelled with vicarious pride. "Indeed she does. How does a week from Sunday sound?"

"Sounds fine to me."

"We'll see you then, Caitlin. Take care, now. Don't get up. I'll run back and get my car." He kissed me quickly on the cheek, and left.

* * * * *

I sat in the Blethering Place after Sandy had gone, feeling depressed and anxious. I flexed my shoulder. It still hurt, but not nearly as much as yesterday. While I was checking myself over, I swallowed a few times and realized that sore throat was gone. Must have been the vitamin C. Or all the excitement of getting shot.

The waitress refilled my coffee cup, and I tried my best to avoid thinking about Tonia. Or Val. Or Tonia and Val. Or, ye gods, Tonia and Caitlin. Charity from Tonia was something I did not need.

Outside the window a young couple hugged goodbye. She pecked him on the cheek, but he pulled her back, kissing her with great thoroughness in full view of the entire tea room. Men. I shook my head. They baffled me. They were about as alien as beings from Arcturus. And, from what I could glean from infrequent conversations with heterosexual women on that subject, the inscrutability of men was a truism. Freud and his rhetorical interrogative about women be damned: what do *men* want? I've never been able to figure it out. The more I learn about them, the more truly alien they seem. Men and women who live together astonish me.

Boring even myself with these musings, I paid the bill, and walked to my car. I checked my watch—just after ten. Time to pay a visit to my friend Francis, a very useful fellow who bragged, quite justifiably I feared, that he could "get anything on anybody." I had precious little time to spare on nonessential activities, but the memory of Baxter Buchanan's eyes, the feeling that I needed to know more about him, just wouldn't leave me. I was certain he wasn't mixed up in this blackmail mess—after all, it was his wife who was one of the victims. But he was guilty of *something* all right—terrorizing his own wife, if nothing else. Maybe Francis could dig out some tasty tidbit that Val could use to blackmail her way out of Baxter's clutches. We'd see. I chuckled, thinking of Francis. When he heard who I wanted him to ferret information on, he'd be in electronic heaven.

* * * * *

107

Francis Poe lived in a barely furnished apartment just off Cook Street in James Bay, not far from the sea. I rang his bell, and a whispery voice asked me to identify myself. Francis is so melodramatic.

"Caitlin Reece," I told him. "No games, Francis. I don't have time."

"All right, all right," he said irritably. "You're sure no fun today."

He buzzed me up, and I heard the bolts and locks being thrown from halfway down the hall. Francis is a very careful person. He has to be. He's Victoria's underground intelligence king.

After he let me in, I had to wait while he reversed the procedure with all the locks. "So go on in to the machines if you're in such a bloody rush," he said testily. "I'm tempted to charge you extra for being such a stick-in-the-mud."

He was going to be difficult, I could see that. I sat down at a table stacked with electronic gear, and Francis came to sit beside me. I thought again how improbably innocent he looked. If you passed him on the street you might think him a kid going to choir practice. About five-five, he was fair-haired, rosy-cheeked, and looked about sixteen. Actually he was my age, and as ruthless as a shark.

"What's it going to be today, Caitlin?"

"You'll love it, Francis," I said enthusiastically, hoping to distract him from thoughts of his fee. "Baxter Buchanan."

He smiled sweetly. "I don't have a file on him."

Oh hell. This *was* going to be expensive. I thought briefly of trying to find the information myself, but abandoned the idea. There just wasn't time. I wanted to wrap this case up by the weekend, and get Val, the letters, the blackmailer, the burglars, and yes, even Tonia, out of my life. And Francis was the expert. Using information available out there in the data jungle, information being amassed by credit bureaus, newspapers, civil servants, city hall recordkeepers, insurance companies, hospitals, schools, the military—Francis could ferret out the best hidden secrets. He claimed he could prepare a dossier on anyone by simply understanding the system and knowing where to dig. He was probably right—his finished products were so complete they scared me. He maintained there was no such thing as a closed source, and he used whatever tools were necessary to get information—flattery, bribes, lies, and, most effective of all, purloined computer database passwords. Much as I hated to admit it, Francis was worth the heart-stopping fees he charged. "How much, Francis?" I asked wearily.

He smiled again, and I noticed how sharp his incisors were. "For you, because we're friends, a thousand. Half in advance."

I exploded. "Jesus, Francis! Is this because I didn't humor you at the door? Damn it, I told you I'm short of time!"

He sulked. "You're so emotional, Caitlin. Do you let your clients see you like this? I hardly think so. No," he said, smiling angelically, "developing a file on the Honorable Baxter Buchanan will be a little more difficult than developing one on," he looked me up and down appraisingly, "Caitlin Reece, say."

"Okay, okay." I pulled out my wallet and counted out five one-hundred dollar bills. Francis always insists on being paid in cash. "When?" I demanded, waving the bills under his nose.

"Monday."

I hooted. "Out of the question. It has to be sooner."

He pouted. "Sunday night."

"No way. Earlier."

"Caitlin, I just can't do it any sooner. You're not my only client, you know."

"Then no deal."

He pretended to think. "Well . . . maybe a little earlier. Saturday, say?"

"Saturday before noon."

"After noon," he said, firmly.

I scowled. I didn't like it, but it would have to do.

He unbent a little. "Tell me what sort of thing you're looking for, and maybe I can phone you earlier with a partial report."

Now that was more like it. "I'm not sure," I told him truthfully, "but I have a feeling it'll be something . . . odd. Something disturbing. And probably something pretty well buried in Buchanan's background. He is a public figure now, after all."

Francis' eyes sparkled. "Caitlin, you want some dirt!"

"That's it, Francis. Dirt. And the sooner the better."

He bounced to his feet and showed me to the door. The lock ritual was repeated, and he ushered me out. "Dirt," he repeated enthusiastically. "You know, Caitlin, that's my favorite kind of job. I'd have only charged you five hundred if you'd told me that up front. And been nicer. I'm going to get on this right away, you silly girl."

I bared my teeth at him, but he slammed the door. "Saturday!" I yelled. "Before noon, you little blood sucker!"

There was no reply. Francis the ferret was already at work.

* * * * *

After a quick coffee at a fast food drive-through, I decided to pay a visit to Malcolm and Yvonne's store. I checked my watch. Just about two. Perhaps I might happen upon that maven of monetary acumen Oliver Renbo, expounding the ethical purity of the Rainbow Fund. Or maybe he had a bridge to sell today. I found a spot for my MG in a green zone, and went inside.

At the back, the little cafe was empty, save for a wispily bearded young man who was examining the dregs of his soup as if for clues. I sighed. I could have used a few clues myself.

"Hi, Caitlin," Yvonne said as I slid onto a stool at the counter.

"I'll have the soup," I told her. The chalkboard said it was cream of broccoli. I figured it would probably do no damage that a visit to McDonald's wouldn't undo. "Where's the financier?" I asked.

"Funny you should ask," she said, putting a large bowl of steaming soup in front of me. "Today was the first time in ages he hasn't been in."

Oho, I thought. Maybe the inquiries I'd asked Virginia Silver to make were shaking his tree a little. Perhaps he'd decided to pack up his scheme and go elsewhere. I hoped so. "Well," I told Yvonne, "I'll have some information for you soon. Sit tight." I looked around. "Where's Malcolm?"

"Just popped out the University ticket office for a minute."

"Oh, who's coming?"

She gave me an eager smile. "Tonia Konig. You know, the nonviolence lady you brought here the other day. Malcolm was thrilled to meet her."

I almost choked on my soup.

"Sunday afternoon she's speaking at the McPherson Auditorium. Malcolm and I want to make sure we get tickets. It's going to be televised." She sighed. "I really admire that woman."

Well, Tonia *did* say that she had a talk to deliver on Sunday. I wondered if I should tell Yvonne that the admirable Dr. Konig was even now ensconced in my spare room, thinking nonviolent thoughts. I decided against it. "Mmm," I said noncommittally. "Should be interesting."

"Malcolm's getting a few extra tickets," she said tentatively. "Would you like to come?"

I furrowed my brow and pretended to think. "Sunday, Sunday, hmm. Nope, I don't think I can make it. Thanks for asking, though." Ye gods. Tonia would probably sniff out my heretical presence in the audience and order me out of the auditorium. Thug, begone! And on TV, too. I felt sure of this, despite the fact that we had shared a bed last night. Sort of. No thanks. If there ever was oil and water, it was us. Besides, I figured by Sunday I'd be ready for about twenty-four consecutive hours of sleep which I intended to precede with a few hours spent abusing alcohol, reading Shakespeare's sonnets, and listening to Bach. Simultaneously. How Tonia expected to be ready for Sunday I had no idea. Fortunately, that wasn't my problem. Saturday was.

* * * * *

I made a quick trip to the Oak Bay photo shop, and, on my way back to the car, a stop at the Back Alley Deli for muffins. I bought another half pound of shaved ham just in case Tonia had eaten the last lot, added a container of potato salad to the order, and dashed back across Oak Bay Avenue to my car. Taking a quick look at the photos, I shrugged. They were simply pictures of people. Well, I had hopes that Tonia could help me identify them. I had a pretty good theory worked out to explain them. And if I was wrong? I sighed. Well then, I'd simply have to formulate a different hypothesis.

Tonia's door was still closed when I came back, busy sounds of typing emanating from inside the room. I knocked quietly.

"Yes?" Her voice was flat, noncommittal.

"Sorry to bother you, but I need your help for a few minutes."

Silence. "All right."

I must admit to more than a small degree of nervousness as I waited for her door to open. Now was certainly the time to talk about last night, but what in God's name could I say? Thanks but no thanks?

She opened the door and gave me one of her long looks. Despite my best intentions, I began to have difficulty breathing. Good grief. Perhaps I should reconsider my hasty decision to decline the good doctor's advances. As St. Augustine said, "Lord, make me pure, but not yet." With difficulty, I reined in my lascivious thoughts. Business first. "Why don't we go on into the living room?" I suggested. "I'm going to make a sandwich and get a beer. In the meantime, you could take a look a the photos in the brown envelope. On the coffee table. Want a snack?"

"No thanks," she said, turning away from me finally.

Repo put in an appearance as I was piling ham on rye bread for my sandwich. He sat politely on the counter, salivating, looking eloquently at the meat. My reluctance to share with Repo was not due to the fact that I wanted to keep the ham for myself. Well, not entirely. Ham isn't good for cats, Yvonne says. Pork fat molecules are larger than average, and though they're degraded during digestion, they're still big. When I learned this, I had a vivid picture of humongous molecules of ham fat making log jams in Repo's tiny arteries, and I realized I hadn't been doing him any favors feeding him tidbits of ham and bacon. Most of the time I can harden my heart and think of his arteries. Today, I felt weak. Also, he was drooling on the counter. So, I gave in.

Tonia looked up in perplexity from the pile of photos as I sat on the couch beside her, depositing sandwich and beer on the coffee table. "Why do you have pictures of these people?" she asked.

"Beats me," I said, licking mustard off my finger. "Why, do you know them?"

"Yes, I do," she replied in amazement. "They're my colleagues."

Now we were getting somewhere. "All of them?"

"Yes. I only know a dozen of them personally, but the other seven I recognize. Did you take these pictures?"

I decided to level with her. "No. I found them in a file in the house on Redfern Street."

"Redfern? You mean the house you . . . "

"Broke into," I supplied, a little impatient with her squeamishness. "Two days ago. But I didn't find these in our friend Harrington's belongings. They were in the closet of a kid named Lester Baines. He's a journalism student."

She shook her head. "I don't understand. Maybe he took the photos for a journalism assignment."

"Possibly. But I don't think so."

"Oh?" she demanded. "Are you sure you're not just, well, letting your imagination run away with you?"

I pulled Sandy's computerized hot sheet out of the envelope and scanned it quickly. Then I passed it to Tonia. "Here's a list of people who reported burglaries in the last six months, along with a list of property stolen. How many of your friends there" I gestured to the pile of photos, "are on the list?"

She read it quickly, then handed it back to me. "All of them. Every one." She raked her hair quickly. "Caitlin, what's going on here?"

I took a swig of beer and launched into my theory. "James Harrington, Lester Baines, and Mark Jerome are students at U Vic. To help finance their education they've taken up burglary. I don't know how the victims are selected, but Baines takes photos of them at their homes and studies their patterns of living. When they come and go, that sort of thing. Then, when they know the victims won't be at home, the kids break in and help themselves. The house on Redfern Street looks like an electronics warehouse."

"Then they're the ones who took the letters!"

"I think so."

"And they're the ones doing the blackmailing."

I shrugged. "The evidence points in that direction, but my guess is that they're not behind it."

114

"Why not? Who else could it be?"

"Why not? Because the crimes don't usually go together. Blackmailers are a slimy lot. Burglars are usually a whole different kettle of fish. And it feels odd to me that these college kids would climb into that kind of sewer." I took a bite of sandwich, chewed, and swallowed. "As for who else it could be, I don't know. But there are only two possibilities. Either Harrington and company *are* the blackmailers, or they aren't. If they aren't, then they passed the letters to someone else."

"But who? And how will you find out?"

I finished the last of my sandwich and beer. "The easy way. I'll ask them."

Tonia gaped. "Just like that?"

"Well, not quite. I'm going to cut one of them out of the herd. Run him to ground. Apply a little pressure. Then we'll see what happens."

"What do you think will happen?"

I considered this. "They're just kids. My guess is whoever I lean on will panic. If I'm lucky, he'll give me the blackmailer."

"And if there is no one else? If the boys are doing the blackmailing?"

I smiled. "Then I've got them. I'm sure they'll be willing to forget all about the letters in exchange for my forgetting that they have a house full of stolen merchandise."

Tonia looked at me incredulously. "What? You won't report them to the police?"

"Certainly not," I told her. "I want the job done properly. Besides," I reminded her, "I thought Val was eager to keep the police out of this."

Tonia nodded. "Yes. She was adamant. She figured it would be sure to leak out."

"All right then," I told her, getting up to take my dishes to the kitchen. "Let me do this my way. My shoulder was twinging; I gobbled six aspirin and went back into the living room.

Tonia came to meet me in the entrance foyer. "Your shoulder seems much better today," she said softly.

I nodded, momentarily tongue-tied.

"Caitlin, about last night," she said, beating me to it.

I shook my head. "This really isn't the best time to talk about it," I told her. She gave me one scorching, unmistakable look, and I just gave in. Finally, I did what I had been wanting to do for days. I reached out and ran my hand down that glossy wing of hair, my fingers registering that it felt as silky as I had fantasized it would. She put her hand over mine and we stood like that, one foot apart. What rotten timing. "I have to go," I said. "I really do. I'm not sure when I'll be back. But we can talk then. All right?"

"All right," she said quietly.

"Thanks for being there last night," I said.

"You're quite welcome," she replied, giving me a megawatt smile.

"I really do have to go," I said, aware that I was repeating myself.

She took her hand away from mine. "I know."

I took a deep breath and turned my back on her. Walking to my MG was one of the least appealing things I had done recently. I slammed the door in frustration and backed out onto Monterey. Now I had another reason for wanting to wrap this up. Saturday was only two days away—surely I could wait until then, I told myself. Maybe not, I answered, gunning the motor. Maybe not.

Chapter 10

I found him in the Journalism Department's drafting lab, sitting on a high stool working with an Exacto knife, laying out columns of print. A tall, thin young man with aviator glasses, a head of tousled sandy hair, and a worried frown. I recognized him as one of the two boys I'd seen in the Buick wagon Monday night. The department's secretary had been extremely helpful when I told her I was Baines' sister, trying to find Lester to bring him to the bedside of our gravely ill mother. Sometimes a little lie is necessary to serve a greater truth. A sleazy rationalization, but mine own.

"Lester," I said as I came up beside him.

"Yes?" he said, looking up with a vaguely apprehensive expression.

I held up the photo of Tonia he had taken, and as soon as he saw it he turned the color of putty.

"Where . . . how . . . who *are* you?"

"Someone who isn't going to roll over and play dead." I assumed my most menacing expression. "You're in big trouble, Lester."

"What do you want?" he whispered, gripping the edges of the drafting table.

"The truth."

He looked down at the neatly cut columns of print as if for inspiration. Finding none, he nodded weakly.

I walked him to the cafeteria, bought us both some coffee, and found a table in the corner. He looked unhappy and nervous. I couldn't say I blamed him.

"I don't know the right questions to ask," I told him, "so why don't you just talk."

He nodded. "I knew this would happen someday," he said, his lower lip trembling. "I'm glad it has. I don't want to do it any more." He closed his eyes. "At first it was just a joke. I took a bunch of pictures of my professors—it's easy to find out where they live. It was fun taking candid shots. But then things got . . . out of hand."

"Out of hand? How?"

"It was Harrington," he said with hatred in his voice. "Him and Farkas. They thought up the whole thing. My job was to take pictures of the profs—the ones Victor lined up for us to hit—and get their routines down pat. Then, when we knew they'd be away, Harrington and Jerome would go in and strip the places." He swallowed half his coffee in a single gulp. "I wanted to stop. I begged them to stop. Or at least to let me out of it. But Farkas kept telling me I was in too deep."

So far, his story matched my suppositions. Except for one item. "Farkas who?" I asked him.

"Farkas. Victor Farkas." Ah, the Victor of the photo file.

"Who is he? Another student?"

Lester shook his head, eager for me to get it all straight, clearly relieved to be getting this off his chest. "No, he's not a student." He looked around fearfully, as if the dreaded Farkas might materialize like an evil genie. "He's Chief of Maintenance."

Chief of Maintenance. Wonderful. Presumably, he had access to all the faculty offices. And in between repairing the professors' air conditioners and replacing light bulbs, he could—what? Ask them when they were taking holidays? Doubtful.

"So how did that help him pick out the houses to burgle?"

Lester looked embarrassed and adjust his glasses. "He just looked around. Usually the profs had out-of-town appointments written in their calendars."

"I see. Enterprising fellow. But then how did you—pardon me, they—get into the houses?"

"Keys," Lester told me. "Victor made impressions of any keys he could find. Harrington and Jerome never had to break in."

"Nice," I said. "So when did your business turn into blackmail?"

He looked as if he was about to cry. "With the last burglary. Dr. Konig. Harrington found the letters just by accident. He gave them to Victor, and he was real excited. He carried them around with him for days. That was pretty weird, I can tell you. Then out of the blue he announced that we were going to help him blackmail her."

"So why is he trying to scare her to death first?"

Lester swallowed, the sharp bulge of his Adam's apple clearly visible in his throat. I tried not to feel sorry for him. "Because he's like that," Lester told me, almost whispering. "He's . . . mean. And . . . he's got this thing about women. He just hates them. Calls them the worst names you can imagine. Says they just ruin good men."

There was something wrong here, and I wondered if Lester had picked up on it. Tonia certainly wasn't ruining any men. And from what I had gathered, most of the campus knew it.

"Does he know Dr. Konig?" I asked him.

Lester shook his head. "Not personally. He'd done work for her, though."

"Of course. But as far as you know he doesn't have any particular grudge against her?" I decided to be tactful. "Her philosophy? Her lifestyle?"

"Oh," he said. "You mean because she's a lesbian?"

Good boy. I owed it to Tonia that he be the one to say it. "Right."

Another head shake. "Hell, everyone knows *that*," he informed me, shrugging. "She's such a good teacher, no one cares."

I let that one go by, glad, however, to see such reasonableness in the young. Valerie needed supporters like this kid, too. "I'm glad you think that, Lester," I told him, "but what about friend Victor? Isn't it a little illogical that he should hate lesbians—they're not ruining any good men."

Lester looked up, surprised by the question. "Yeah, I thought about that, too. It doesn't make sense, does it?" He shrugged. "He hasn't ever said anything about lesbians that I recall. Not specifically. I don't think he makes a distinction. They're all women to him so they're all rotten."

What? That was ridiculous. Well, maybe we'd come back to that point later.

"Who shot at Tonia, Lester?"

I thought the kid was going to run for it, and I poised myself to grab him. His lower lip began to tremble again, and he moaned. "Harrington."

"Busy boy, isn't he?"

Lester nodded miserably. "Farkas said to shoot out her window, shake her up good."

120

I sat back, thinking. So the intention hadn't been to wound Tonia; Harrington had just been a bad shot. My shoulder suddenly throbbed, as if in its own anger. "How did you guys get mixed up with Victor, anyhow?"

Lester laughed bitterly. "He's our landlord. He lives in the house right next to us on Redfern, so he's always hanging around. He's a real creep. And since you brought the subject up, I'll tell you what I think. I think he's sick."

I raised an eyebrow. "Sick how?"

"Well," Lester said, blushing, "I mean, no one cares about people's sexual preferences anymore, right? We're all entitled to do our own thing."

I smiled. A little naive, but well meant nonetheless. I was getting a little tired of this beating around the bush, though. "Lester, are you trying to say that Victor is gay?"

He squirmed. "Not exactly."

I sighed. This was like pulling teeth. "So what is he then? Not a heterosexual, surely."

"God, no."

"Come on, Lester! What?"

Lester looked embarrassed. "I think he'd like to be gay. You know, do something about the way he feels about men."

So he was a latent homosexual. Very interesting. Thoughts of blackmail began to dance in *my* head. "What makes you think that?" I asked Lester.

"Well," Lester said, lowering his voice, "sometimes we all watch TV together, and he just can't seem to keep his mouth shut. Every woman is awful, but every man is terrific. And when it comes to married men whose wives are cheating on them—" he shook his head. "It's too weird. He gets so caught up in these programs—he seems to think they're *real*. Yeah, cheating wives drive him a little crazy." He seemed to remember the thrust of my question and changed course a little. "Him and Harrington hang out a lot together. They go to the gym, go over to Vancouver for the weekend, rent a boat, go fishing together — like that. I think he likes Harrington a whole lot." He shrugged. "That's all. Well, except for one other thing. He bores us to death with his war stories—I almost forgot about them."

"War stories?"

"Yeah. He can sit for hours telling us about the good old days." Lester shrugged "He was in some bomber squadron, and he remembers every mission they flew. They were finally shot down over France somewhere, close to the end of the war, and Victor saved the pilot's life. The rest of the crew burned to death. That pilot was Victor's hero, I guess. The perfect man."

Interesting. But I failed to see how this information could be useful. I sat back, frowning. If cheating wives drove him crazy, why wasn't he going after Val, then? Why was it Tonia who was pushing his crazy button?

"You said Victor carried the letters around with him for a while. Do you know where they are now?"

Lester shook his head. "I have no idea."

It was too much to hope for. Well, time to go. But before I did, I'd have to make sure that Lester kept his mouth shut.

"Lester, you've told me enough to get yourself put in jail for years. Victor's right, you know—you are in just as deep as the rest of them."

He nodded miserably.

"But I may be able to help you."

He looked at me skeptically, not wanting to hope. "How? And why should you, anyhow?"

"Why? To have an ally in the enemy camp," I told him honestly. "As for how, well, you'll just have to trust me."

He continued to look at me, and now I saw something else in his eyes. Fear. And regret. He was already sorry he'd talked to me. After all, what could I do for him?

"Listen, Lester," I told him. "Victor Farkas, James Harrington, and Mark Jerome are all going down for the

122

count. Make no mistake about that. I will personally see to it. I haven't decided yet whether to turn them over to the police, or . . . " I began to give vent to my imagination, " . . . to take them for a boat ride. Or maybe they'll have a car accident. Tonia and Val are my friends. Are you following me?"

He nodded. "Who *are* you?" he asked again.

I bared my teeth in a feral grin. "Just someone who doesn't like to see other people victimized." I wrote my phone number on a piece of paper and held it out to him. When he reached for it, I crumpled it in my fist. He looked up at me fearfully. "I want to know we have an understanding, Lester," I told him. "In return for letting you walk away from this, I want you to try your best to find out for me why Victor has it in for Dr. Konig, and where the letters are. And I need to know this by Saturday morning. Oh, and I expect you to let me know if he has any other nasty surprises planned. Agreed?"

He opened his mouth to protest, saw the look on my face, and thought better of it. "I can let you know about anything weird he might have planned. But what if I can't find out the other things?" he asked me weakly.

I shrugged. "Then I don't owe you anything, do I?"

He closed his eyes and shook his head. "No."

"So try hard, Lester. You wouldn't like it in prison. You're too pretty."

He looked at me in horror and I hated myself. I opened my fist and let him take the piece of paper. "Saturday, Lester."

"All right," he said. "I promise. I'll do my best."

I believed he would. I also believed his best wouldn't be good enough. I would still have to do this on my own.

I walked him back to class, noting the location of a bank of pay phones on the first floor of the Journalism building. But although I sat across the student lounge from the phones, lurking behind a paper for the better part of half an hour, Lester did not show up to use them. That heartened me. It

123

meant that he was more afraid of me than of Victor. Maybe he *would* be useful after all. But the kid was a nervous wreck. I only hoped he wouldn't come apart at the seams before Saturday.

* * * * *

I drove home feeling a bit panicked. Time's winged chariot, as the poet said, was hurrying near. And my thoughts had described one enormous circle—a zero. The concept might be fascinating to mathematicians, but it was a big fat nothing to me. I was right back where I had been Monday night. Well, maybe not quite. I now knew who the blackmailer was, but I didn't quite know how to stop him in time. I could always turn Francis the ferret loose on him, but not before Saturday. Damn. The prospect of being able to blackmail Farkas was a sweet one. I was tempted to content myself with just getting the letters back. With them, Farkas held all the cards in this game. Without them, well, we might be able to negotiate. However, the question of Farkas' motive was bothering me. A lot.

I shuddered, recalling what Lester had said about him, An iron pumper, was he? So I could forget about any ideas of trying to intimidate him. And a woman hater, too. I groaned. That was going to make him a tough nut to crack. And I wasn't feeling especially tough myself these days.

God, I'd been dense. I had concentrated on the kids. Why? Because they had been right under my nose. Observant, aren't you, Caitlin, I chastised myself. The stocky, grizzle-haired man who had climbed out of the Buick Tuesday afternoon on Redfern had been right under your nose, too. And you'd even entertained some suspicions about him. Dumb, Caitlin, dumb. Well, I had a little time left. I certainly knew how I'd better use it. I checked my watch. Mid-afternoon. Time enough. I needed to make a quick trip home—I had no intentions of tangling with the muscle-bound Victor unarmed.

And maybe Tonia could shed some light on why Victor was after her. Although I sensed I would have to be gentle with her. Not that she was fragile in the way Val was—not at all. Tonia had guts, all right. It was simple consideration: no one wants to be told they're a weirdo's victim. I intended to present her with the facts and let her draw the conclusion for herself. And in the course of doing so, perhaps something bright would occur to her. I hoped so. Because nothing bright was occurring to me.

I maneuvered the MG through traffic, brooding on Victor's motive. Discounting pure craziness, which just didn't seem right to me, there seemed to be only three possibilities.

Number one. Victor was doing what he was doing because he was a misogynist—he just had it in for women. But that didn't fit with what Lester had told me. Farkas hated women because they ruined men. And he hated cheating wives in particular. That should have let Tonia off the hook right there. Therefore, this hypothesis was wrong.

I sighed. Number two. Victor hated lesbians. Tonia was a lesbian, and he was taking his ire out on her. Nope. Again, that didn't square with Lester's description of Farkas. He had no specific antipathy for lesbians. So this hypothesis also wouldn't wash.

Number three. The money. Farkas saw the opportunity to soak these two errant broads for a small fortune. I frowned. Maybe. Money *was* a powerful motive. Hell, maybe it was the money. That would explain a lot.

But it didn't explain why Farkas wasn't pursuing Val with the same singleminded energy as he was Tonia. I pounded the steering wheel in frustration. There was something I wasn't seeing here, and it was making *me* a little crazy. I needed help.

* * * * *

125

To my surprise, Tonia was sitting in the living room reading, her long legs gracefully tucked up under her, a mug of coffee on the table. Well, why not? Everyone deserved a break now and then. I felt envious.

"You're back soon," she remarked.

I crossed the living room and paused outside my bedroom door. "Wait right there," I told her, then quickly went in to get what I needed. My self control in the presence of Tonia Konig was fast fraying. Having her poised in the bedroom door would not have been conducive to professional conduct.

"I've been thinking that I owe you an apology," she said as I returned to the living room.

"Oh?" I said cautiously, taking a chair at what I judged to be a safe distance from her.

"Yes." She looked at me in embarrassment. "I know you're doing your best for me. And Val. Directing my anger toward you was completely inappropriate. I'm sorry."

I smiled. "I'll consider that an official apology. I accept. Now, how about if I give you someone appropriate to direct your anger at?"

She looked at me in disbelief. "You don't mean you actually persuaded one of those boys to talk to you?"

I nodded. "Yeah. And you'll be happy to know that I didn't even have to beat on him. The kid has such a guilty conscience he was glad to confess." I frowned. "I only hope he can keep his mouth shut until Saturday."

"What did he tell you?"

"Do you know someone named Victor Farkas?"

She thought for a moment. "I don't think so." Then she sat up straight in her chair. "Wait—yes I do! Farkas is Chief of Maintenance at U Vic. Why?"

"He's the blackmailer," I told her.

"What? But the boys . . . they must be working for him!" She trailed off, thinking. "Last Christmas the heating controls in my office had to be repaired," she told me. "The Chief of

Maintenance himself came over to do it. I thought it was a little odd at the time."

I nodded. "Mmmhmm. And you were out of the office for part of the time when he was there, right?"

"Sure. I had exams to supervise."

She looked at me, comprehension in her eyes. This lady was quick, all right.

"That bastard must have looked through my appointment book! That's how he knew I'd be away in February."

I nodded. "According to the kid I talked to, Victor then made an impression of your house keys, thus sparing the kiddy burglars the trouble of breaking in."

She shook her head. "And the boys found the letters, gave them to him, and—"

"—and here we are," I said.

Then I waited. I wanted her to discover for herself that she, not Val, was his target. Dammit, this just had to make sense. She was silent for a few moments, and I grew impatient. I decided to push her a little. "Let's forget the burglary and concentrate on what happened afterward."

"What do you mean?"

"Well, hasn't there been a lot of unwelcome attention paid you recently?"

She looked at me, her eyes huge. "Go on."

I ticked off the points on my fingers. "It was your picture I found in Lester Baines' files. It was you James Harrington ran down on campus. And it was your window the sniper shot out."

She began to look a little ill.

"That's why you insisted I move in here."

I nodded.

"That's why you haven't been so . . . concerned about Val."

"Right."

"So it isn't Val and me at all. It's me this man is after."

I said nothing.

"God, Caitlin, why? Do you mean he really doesn't want the money? What *does* he want, anyhow? To kill me?"

"No, I don't think so. That bullet was only a .22 and I had a pretty thick jacket on. Also, I stood in one place for a good length of time. He had plenty of time to aim. If he'd wanted to kill me—excuse me, you—he'd have done things differently. No, he just wanted to shoot out your window." I hoped I was right.

"Then what's this all about?"

"I was hoping you could tell me."

"Me? Dammit, Caitlin, you're the investigator!"

I laughed a little bitterly. "Right."

"I don't know why he picked me over Val," Tonia said indignantly. "Not that I'd wish this sort of attention on her, but why me?"

I stood up. Evidently no help was forthcoming here. Ah well.

"Where are you going?" she demanded, a touch of the old belligerence creeping back into her voice. Atta girl, Tonia, I applauded. Get good and mad. It helps hold off the fear.

As for me, I was furious. Why couldn't I figure this out? "I haven't been too bright up until now," I confessed. "I made a big mistake concentrating on the kids. But I intend to redress that error."

"Oh?" she said a little sarcastically. "How?"

"By concentrating on Farkas. He isn't a genius, you know," I told her. "We have that going for us. And most important of all, we have an edge."

"We do? What edge can we possibly have?"

"He doesn't know we're— I'm — coming after him."

She closed her eyes. Well, I couldn't say I blamed her. My performance hadn't been exactly confidence-inspiring so far. She looked at me wearily. "Caitlin, just what—"

"Can *I* do?" I finished the question for her. "Pay a little visit to our friend Farkas."

She looked at me in genuine alarm.

I smiled. "Well, to Farkas' house anyhow."

"Damn him!" she cried. "Damn all of them!"

I walked around the couch and fetched my .357 from where I had put it in the dining room cabinet. Quickly, out of her range of vision, I threaded the holster through my belt loops, buckled it, and took my gun out of its case. Just the sight of its cold, blue steel made me feel better. I checked its ammunition load and replaced the gun in the holster. I walked back around the couch to the front door. "You know," I told her, "damning on its own isn't enough. I'm afraid I don't trust Providence."

"You wouldn't," she said flatly.

"I'm not the trusting type," I said, shrugging. "Sometimes you just have to help Providence along. Besides," I told her, "if you do a job yourself, then you know it's being done properly. Damning is a tricky business. You have to get it just right."

She said nothing, just sat and looked at me as if I, not Farkas, were responsible for this mess. Evidently our temporary truce was over. I shook my head and let myself out of the house, quietly closing the door behind me.

Chapter 11

There was no time for finesse. I just drove up to Farkas' house, parked, and prayed that he hadn't taken a sick day. Now that I was back here on Redfern, I could see that the paint was still peeling off 1074. But it was the little house beside it, 1076, that now interested me. It was a tiny, pebble stuccoed place, hardly more than a cottage, but both yard and house were well cared for. No flowers in the beds, no fresh paint, but the grass had been cut, the weeds kept down, and no obvious repairs seemed needed. A neutral, anonymous house. I patted Smith and Wesson once for reassurance, and walked between the houses to the back door.

The lock was nothing special, and in a minute I was in the kitchen. I closed the door cautiously, making sure it didn't lock behind me, then looked around. I was impressed. Not only was everything neat, it was spotlessly clean. The linoleum was old and scuffed to a faded blue, but it had been freshly scrubbed and waxed. Someone had done some interior decorating recently, and a faint smell of paint lingered in the air. The cupboards, I guessed. They looked shiny and white.

In the living room/dining room was a home gym. There were more weights than I had seen at Nautilus, a bench press, a situp board, some gym mats, and of course, the requisite mirror. I took a look at myself in it and started in surprise—I looked terrible. Pale and drawn, mauve half moons under my eyes. Well, I felt kind of rotten, too. Flexing my shoulder, I grimaced at the Caitlin in the mirror and moved on.

On to the bedroom. It was fanatically neat. The bed had hospital corners, the clothes were carefully aligned in the closet and drawers, and there was no dust anywhere. But the room looked . . . sterile. There wasn't a picture, a photo, or a book anywhere. Nothing to suggest that anyone lived here. A trunk in the corner had V.A. FARCAS stencilled on it, and I hesitated, checking my watch. It was getting late.

Come on, Caitlin, I chided myself, bite the bullet. You've been dragging your ass ever since you came in here. Just get it over with. Why so squeamish? What did you think you'd find here? I shivered, then got a grip on myself. I could do it if I hurried. I knelt, picked the lock, and opened the trunk. The odor of mothballs assailed me. Inside was a stack of clothes—old Canadian Air Force uniforms. My own father had worn uniforms just like these. There were two charcoal grey wool winter uniforms, some blue cotton shirts, one khaki summer uniform, and a khaki shirt. All clean and neatly folded, but well worn. The arm stripes said that V.A. Farkas had been a sergeant. I rooted around in the trunk and uncovered something else. A pile of body building magazines. Big deal.

I dug a little deeper and found a scrapbook. No, two scrapbooks. I hauled them out and began riffling through the

132

first one. It was full of old Air Force pictures. Planes and people. Groups of men lounging around in their undershirts, posing beside a plane that looked like an old F 86. Still other groups of men standing formally in front of a hangar. I shrugged. Exactly like my father's old Air Force photos—mementos of his days with various flight crews. The biggest photo was of four men sitting on the wing of a plane, and another, obviously the pilot, sitting in the cockpit giving the thumbs up sign. Was this the pilot Farkas had rescued? No way to tell. He seemed vaguely familiar, though. I shrugged. Maybe he was a war hero. In the same photo, a much younger Farkas sat on the plane's wing while another crewman held a hand-lettered sign that read *BB's Bomber*. The quintet looked healthy, young, and happy. I signed. Nothing incriminating here. I dried my sweaty palms on my jeans, and opened the next book.

And almost at once, the hair on the back of my neck began to rise. Pages and pages of photos of the same man. Not Farkas—the pilot of the plane I had seen in the last book. This was the loving, or obsessive, cataloguing of a life. I tried to swallow, but my mouth was too dry. Now I knew the name of the plane's pilot. I flipped quickly through the scrapbook. The book was filled with photos and newspaper clippings detailing the career of one person, a person who was obviously very special to Farkas, the B.B. of *BB's Bomber*. Baxter Carlisle Buchanan.

But just what this all meant was something I'd have to ponder later. Or did it mean anything, I wondered. Perhaps it was just a coincidence—one of Farkas' victims just happened to be the wife of someone he admired. I really didn't believe in coincidences like that. They were too unlikely. But what else *could* it be?

I ran out of the house to my car, my eye on my watch. Not quite four. I had one more haunt of Victor's to check out this afternoon.

133

* * * * *

I sat in my MG outside U Vic's administration building parking lot, keeping my eye on Farkas' car. I thought the greater part of wisdom might be to cool my heels here until I saw him drive off. I wouldn't want to pick the lock of his office door only to find him sitting there in the dark like a troll, brooding.

I listened to the radio, read the paper, then went inside to use the ladies' room. I walked around, bought two roast beef sandwiches and a carton of milk from a machine, and had my lunch just inside the building's main entrance where I could see the car. I picked up a copy of the undergraduate student newspaper, the faculty newspaper, and the grad student newspaper, and went back to my car to read. Four-fifty. At five-oh-three Farkas came out, unlocked his car, and got in. Almost simultaneously, Harrington and Jerome came along and joined him. Farkas drove out of the parking lot.

Just after five is a good time to be around administrative offices. There's a lot of confusion and hurrying. No one wants to work any unpaid overtime. So the very rushed young secretary I approached was, while buttoning up, only too happy to give me as short an answer as possible..

"Victor Farkas? Who? Oh, you mean *Vic*. Yeah, sure. His office is in the basement. Right next to the elevator. But he's probably gone. Listen, I've got to run. Why don't you come back tomorrow?"

Right, I thought, and took the stairs. In the basement was a short hall leading to a student lounge with chairs and tables and dispensing machines, and a duplicating center which was just closing. Lining the hall was a bunch of locked doors that said respectively, *Men, Women,* and *V.A. Farkas, Chief of Maintenance.* I went on into the student lounge, got a cup of perfectly vile coffee from one of the machines, and sat in a corner where I could see the whole room. Gradually it emptied as students melted away in search of dinner or evening festivities, except for a kid sacked out on a couch, and another one engrossed in a copy of *PC Magazine*, his back to the door.

The hall was empty, and I had my picks out before I got to Farkas' door. For the ten seconds it took me to pick his lock, I sweated. And then I was in. I closed the door quietly behind me, heart beating hard, and looked around.

It was a perfectly ordinary looking office, maybe fifteen feet square. One window, covered with wire mesh and set high in the wall, gave me not quite enough light to see. I cursed, because in a few minutes I would have to either turn on his office light or use my flashlight. So I worked as fast as I could.

The top of his desk was no help. Work orders, requests for repairs, invoices, all separated into neat piles. The top middle desk drawer was a jumble of paper clips, pencils, BIC pens, erasers, magic markers, rubber bands, staples, and tape. The right-hand top drawer held blank forms, letterhead, envelopes, plain bond, and about half a dozen 10 x 15-inch brown envelopes.

Plain bond and brown envelopes. A small light went on in my brain. I took out the brown envelopes and examined them. In each of the upper left-hand corners was a small dimple, just like the envelopes that had been sent to Tonia and Val. I took one of the sheets of bond between my fingers and held it up to the light. A watermark. The hair on the back of my neck began to lift a little. I took one of the brown envelopes, stuffed a sheet of bond in it, and put it in my pocket. Comparison shopping.

I resumed my search of the desk. In the bottom right-hand drawer were personnel evaluation reports. Top left drawer held a coffee mug, a spoon, a package of Lipton instant chicken soup, and a small jar of MJB coffee. Terrific.

The bottom left-hand drawer was locked. Excited, I picked it, and when I pulled it open, I was acutely disappointed. Well, what had I really expected anyhow? The letters? A signed confession? There was only a bottle of Canadian Club whiskey. I felt like taking a swig.

I locked the drawer, and looked around the office. It was now very late. In the waning light I saw a filing cabinet shoved against one wall and a bookcase against the other. I checked the bookcase first. No luck. It was filled with such tasty tomes as the city and campus phone books, a five-volume set entitled *University Personnel Policy*, and some old folded newspapers.

That left the filing cabinet. By now it was too dark to read anything, so I pulled out my penlight. The lock yielded easily, and shielding the light with my cupped hand, I opened the top drawer. It was filled with old work orders and invoices in individual files from 1979 to 1982. The second drawer contained more of the same, only of a more recent vintage. With the third drawer, however, I hit the jackpot.

I couldn't believe it. I sat on the floor, gingerly opening the 10 x 15 brown envelope that held the letters, and shook them out to make sure. There they were, all six of them. I counted the pages. Twenty-seven, just like the voice on the phone had said. There was nothing else in the drawer.

Scuttling back over to the desk, I opened the stationery drawer, took twenty-seven sheets of bond and put them into white envelopes, then stuffed the whole lot into a new 10 x 15 brown envelope. When I was finished I had a package of about the same size and heft as the letters. I put the new package into the filing cabinet, and closed the drawer. Unless Farkas was addicted to reading the letters every day, only the poorest of luck would reveal the switch.

There was no one in the hall outside Farkas' office, and no one accosted me on the way to my car. As I drove away, the brown envelope containing the letters sat on the seat beside me like a quiescent cobra. I knew I wouldn't feel confident until they were stashed someplace safer than the bottom drawer of *my* filing cabinet.

It was now past six, so I had to abandon the idea of taking them to my bank and caching them in my safe deposit box. The lockers at the airport and bus station were too far away. I thought about my home, my health club, and the trunk of my car, and discarded them all. Ditto for my friends' homes and cars. Then it came to me.

I stopped at a Shopper's Drug Mart, purchased a packet of large mailing envelopes, and ran back to my car.

I was about to stuff the letters into one of the brown envelopes when a little bird of caution spoke to me. Read them, it said. I was appalled at the suggestion. Still, it was not without merit. Perhaps the letters would contain the explanation for Victor's persecution of Tonia. Maybe she had said something that really ticked him off. I locked the MG's doors and started to read.

* * * * *

Half an hour later, I had finished. Feeling vaguely disgusted with myself, I folded the letters thoughtfully and put them into one of the mailing envelopes. Then I just sat there, mulling over what I had read.

They weren't really love letters at all. They were an accounting of the progress of guilt. Val had, as I suspected, succumbed to Tonia's charms (although I gathered that Val, not Tonia, had been the instigator) and had promptly fallen into a fit of remorse. It seemed awfully adolescent to me. Val's letters began by being guilty and self-abnegating, and ended by repudiating the feeling that she had had for Tonia in the first place. Tonia's letters began by being supportive and understanding, and ended by being thoroughly pissed off at Val's foolish denial of what she had felt. The ultimate piece of foolishness, to my mind, had been Val's sending Tonia Shakespeare's Sonnet 147. The Dark Lady Sonnet. I held the page up to the MG's overhead light and read it again.

137

My love is as a fever, longing still
For that which longer nurseth the disease;
Feeding on that which doth preserve the ill,
The uncertain sickly appetite to please.
My reason, the physician to my love,
Angry that his prescriptions are not kept,
Hath left me, and I desperate now approve
Desire is death, which physic did except.
Past cure I am, now Reason is past care,
And frantic-mad with evermore unrest;
My thoughts and my discourse as madmen's are,
At random from the truth vainly express'd;
For I have sworn thee fair, and thought thee bright,
Who are as black as hell, as dark as night.

Pretty heady stuff, I thought. And very disturbing. Again, I hadn't been bright. I had assumed from the one page of the letters Farkas had included, that I knew all I needed to know about them. Wrong. Val, it seemed, had an ax to grind. She evidently thought this horrible thing that had happened to her was all Tonia's fault. Well, perhaps I should have a little chat with Ms. Frazier. Just to clear the air. A tiny spore of suspicion was now germinating in my brain. But first I had to attend to the letters.

Stuffing the blackmail letters into one large mailing envelope, I sealed it shut, and wrote on the outside "Caitlin's letters." Folding the edges a little, I shoved it into another envelope, then wrote a short note explaining what the letters were, and what should be done about them should I fail to come and pick them up. Then I addressed the envelope to Jan on Texada Island, dug a one-dollar stamp out of the glove compartment, and tossed the envelope into the nearest postbox. There. The letters were as safe as I could arrange.

A trip to the phone booth on the corner confirmed one of my suspicions—Val was not able to come to the phone. Her housekeeper simply informed me that Mr. Buchanan and Ms. Frazier had retired early for the evening and did not wish to be disturbed. When pressed, she replied that the happy couple would be leaving tomorrow right after airtime to spend the weekend at Buchanan's farm. I could contact Ms. Frazier at the television studio tomorrow if I wished.

I didn't like this one bit. It wasn't reasonable that Val would arrange to be incommunicado this weekend. She knew as well as Tonia when the blackmailer intended to call. Damn! Had Val arranged this, or was it something over which she had no control? Maybe I'd made yet another mistake in not keeping Val under closer surveillance.

Well, there was no help for it now. I had a more pressing problem—how to call Farkas off. And right now I had no good ideas about that. Something told me, however, that I'd better have a bright idea soon—one that tied this whole thing together—or someone was going to get hurt. Well, shucks, that shouldn't be hard for a big thinker like me. Especially since I'd been so bright about everything up to now. I slammed the MG's door in disgust and floored the accelerator, hearing the tires howl as they spun on the pavement. Better them than me.

* * * * *

I closed the front door to my house as quietly as I could. I had no desire to talk to Tonia. Her ill-concealed lack of confidence earlier today had not exactly endeared her to me. She would want to know what I had found and what I planned to do about it. And whereas I could describe the former, I would have to admit my poverty of ideas about the latter.

Sounds of intermittent typing came from the spare room, so I took a beer from the fridge and went into my bedroom and lay down on my bed in the dark. Repo came to join me, and I cuddled him into the crook of one arm. My arm itched

139

and burned, and I tentatively fingered the sutures. Repo complained, so I tried to lie still. I finished the beer, put the bottle on my night table, and decided to rest for just a moment before I resumed serious thinking.

I yawned, wondering if Tonia and I were now engaged in a battle of wills. There was no doubt that we were attracted to each other, but would either of us be able to put aside our philosophic differences long enough to permit the attraction to flower? I sighed and closed my eyes. Oh well, casual sex is the junk food of the heart, I reminded myself. Sure it is, I replied ruefully as sleep laid its black velvet hands on me and pulled me under.

FRIDAY

Chapter 12

I awakened in a panic. I was lying on my bed, fully dressed, my heart pounding madly. Outside it was daylight. What time *was* it? I checked my clock radio—only eight-thirteen. Thank God. All the pieces of this puzzle rushed into my head like bees returning to the hive. The boy burglars. Vic Farkas. Baxter Buchanan. Val. Tonia. The letters. My brain buzzed. Well, one thing at a time.

I picked up the phone and called Lester Baines. One of his buddies went to fetch him, and I could hear a lot of masculine guffawing at the breakfast table in the background. Obviously Mr. Baines was not exactly a ladies' man.

"Lester, it's me," I told him. "The lady who came to chat with you yesterday."

He made a strangled sound, then quickly recovered. "Yes?" he said in a distinct soprano.

"Come on, Lester, calm down for God's sake. Pretend you're getting a phone call from a nice young lady, not from Khadaffi."

"All right," he replied, his voice falling at least an octave. "Er, how are you?"

"Atta boy. Try to act natural. Can we talk on this phone?"

"Um, I don't think that's such a good idea."

"Hmm. Can you meet me somewhere?"

"Well, all right. But I have to be at class at ten."

"Lester, relax. What I have to say won't make you late." Such diligence.

"Okay," he said with a marked lack of enthusiasm. "Where?"

"Just walk out to Oak Bay Avenue in twenty minutes. I'll pick you up on the corner."

He sighed resignedly. "I'll be there."

* * * * *

He was on the corner right on time, and apparently alone, but I drove down Redfern just to check. He had kept his mouth shut after all, it seemed. I honked the horn and he hurried over. I drove to British Fish 'N Chips at The Junction, and parked.

"Had breakfast, Lester?" I asked as we perused menus.

He looked a little ill. "No, but I think I'll wait and get something on campus. You aren't going to eat this stuff for *breakfast*, are you?"

"Sure," I said cheerfully. "As Mark Twain said: 'Eat what you please and let the food fight it out inside.' "

He ordered only coffee. I, however, had the halibut special. Halfway through my cole slaw, I sprang the news on him.

144

"I found the letters."

His surprise was slapstick. "You did? Where?"

"In your friend Victor's office."

"Then I'm off the hook, right?"

"Not so fast, Lester. You have to do *something* for me. That was our deal."

His shoulders sagged in disappointment, but he nodded.

"All right, Lester. Here it is. I want you to take that trusty camera of yours and photograph all the stolen property in your house. Make sure you get the serial numbers. I want the negatives developed and in my hands by Saturday morning. That's tomorrow."

He gulped, then opened and closed his mouth several times, reminding me unpleasantly of a fish drowning in air. "But that's no time at all! How can I—"

"Just do it. How is up to you."

He closed his eyes. Perhaps he was invoking the god of photography. If he wasn't, I felt he should consider it.

"That's the easy part," I told him.

"Oh, God," he said faintly. "What else."

"Farkas is probably going to want to collect his money tomorrow night. While he and I are transacting business, I want you to have a little chat with your friends. You're going to have to be very persuasive, Lester."

"Why?" he squeaked.

"Because by the time Farkas gets back, I want you busy little burglars to have returned all the stolen property to its rightful owners."

"Oh nooo," he moaned. "But, but, um, even if I could persuade them, we don't know who the property came from."

I handed him a list with two columns on it—serial numbers and descriptions down one side, names and addresses down the other. "Now you do."

"They'll never listen to me," he whispered. "Especially not Harrington."

"Make them listen, Lester. Because I'm going to arrange for the police to meet Mr. Farkas at your house tomorrow night," I lied shamelessly. "Do you think he's going to protect the three of you? Dream on. He'll finger you for the burglaries so fast it'll make your heads spin. But if there *are* no stolen goods there . . . "

"I get it," he said. "So you're going to turn Farkas in for blackmailing Dr. Konig?"

"Yup," I assured him. While it wasn't strictly true, it was close enough. "And I think you kids deserve another chance. I'm inclined to be generous—I'll let the three of you walk away from this. All you have to do is give the goods back."

He swallowed nervously. "That's all? Well, maybe I *can* convince them. In fact, I'm sure of it." He began to sound more confident.

I decided to dispense a piece of unsought advice. "And if I were you, I sure wouldn't take the stolen property back myself. I'd call cabs, or use delivery companies. Some of your victims might recognize you from campus. Also, I'd pack up my belongings and move out tomorrow night. After talking to me, Farkas is going to be in one very foul mood. When he returns home to find all his stolen property gone, even Victor will begin to suspect that all might not be right with the world. And if the police were to be a wee bit late," I embellished, "he might have time to take his ire out on those around him." Actually I *was* afraid for the kids. Especially Lester.

Lester looked dazed and sick. "Right."

I was beginning to worry about him already. "Are you taking all this in?"

He nodded.

"All right. Do you still have my number?"

He patted his shirt pocket. I was touched. He was carrying it next to his heart.

"Call me if there seems to be any problems. Otherwise, you'll meet me here tomorrow at, say, ten. With the pictures."

"Okay."

"Want some more coffee?"

He shook his head.

"Let's go then. You've got a class to get to. Have a nice day, Lester."

* * * * *

I drove down Foul Bay Road to the water. The ocean looked troubled today—grey and choppy. Across the Straits of Juan de Fuca, the Olympics were almost invisible—grey, hulking giants, lurking behind cloaks of clouds. It was not an inspiring sight. I decided to do something to make myself feel better, even though it meant a long drive out of town up the Saanich Peninsula. If I were going to have to stand toe to toe with Victor Farkas, I wanted help. Fortunately, I knew where to get it.

* * * * *

Gray Ng was not at home. I hadn't expected she would be. But I needed to leave a message, and at the Ng farmhouse there is no phone. As I drove up the hill and parked, Gray's aunt came out to greet me. Couldn't I come in for tea, dinner, drinks, or whatever I might like? I was touched. Auntie remembered me.

Three years ago I had helped Gray buy the property—a rundown farmhouse and a quarter section of land that no one wanted. Literally just off the boat from Vietnam, Gray and her family were lambs to be fleeced, and the realtor who had listed the property saw Gray coming a mile away. Overnight the price of the property tripled and poor Gray thought she was obligated to pay. Fortunately a lawyer in the Vietnamese community in Victoria knew Virginia. I paid the owner of the property a nocturnal visit, and persuaded him to be reasonable. It didn't take much persuasion. Gray was able to take possession the next day, at the originally listed price. Her family loved the land, and at once began to grow flowers and vegetables. Now they shipped daffodils and tulips all over Canada.

Gray herself, however, was one of the strangest people I have ever met. Spooky. She loved animals, and for a time worked at a veterinary hospital in Saanich. However, her strange ideas about interspecies communication eventually lost her her job. She tried out her theories once too often on the patients, and her boss panicked. I've seen Gray at work a few times, and if there ever was anyone who could talk to the animals, it's Gray. Ferocious dogs become gentle with her; frightened cats, tractable; skittish horses, calm.

And of course, during the time Gray worked at the vet hospital, she acquired her own collection of unwanted animals. Next to her cats, my favorites were a pair of female Great Danes — the brindled kind — that someone brought into the vet hospital to be destroyed. They were savage and uncontrollable, the owner claimed. Gray took them home with her that night, worked her magic on them, and brought them back tame as lambs the next morning. That was the straw that broke her boss's back. He declared, so Gray's aunt told me, that she was a "damned Asian witch" and ordered her off his property. Knowing Gray, she probably just smiled and went.

Several times, when I have needed to seem exceptionally persuasive, I have asked Gray to borrow "the girls" as she calls the Danes. Sometimes she has accompanied me; sometimes not. When I have the girls, I always wonder who Gray considers is really taking care of whom.

I figured that Saturday night would be a night I would like to have the girls along. I wrote a note and asked Auntie to have Gray get in touch with me. There was a phone over at the flower packing barn—Auntie assured me that Gray would call. There are very few things one can count on in this world, but the word of an Ng was one of them. I drove down the hill from the farmhouse feeling that things were slowly coming together.

* * * * *

On the way home from Gray's house, I got caught in the tail end of commuter traffic. Resignedly, I crawled along until I found the McDonald's on the highway just out of town. With guilty anticipation, I pulled over.

Spotting a pay phone just outside the restaurant, I ran over. Business first. As I had feared, Francis' number was busy. Well, he was probably hooked up via his modem with some hapless host computer, electronically breaking and entering. I certainly hoped he was finding something useful. My mental itch about Baxter Buchanan was demanding to be scratched.

I hung up and went back to my car. As I ordered from the drive-through, I thought fancifully that one could probably navigate one's way across the country using the Golden Arches as ancient navigators did stars. Fortunately, my supper arrived just then, and I abandoned abstraction for the reality of junk food.

Chapter 13

I fought my way up out of sleep, yelling my head off. It was Aunt Fiona's Dark Lady. She was shuffling and twitching her way up the cellar steps after me, making a horrid breathy cackling sound.

Caitlin, she whispered, *Caitlin . . . at last.*

Paralyzed with fear, I stood on the top step and waited for her.

After I had shouted myself awake, I sat on the edge of the bed, soaked with sweat, and ran my hands through my damp hair. Brother. Many more dreams like that and I'd be ready for a padded room.

I changed into a dry sweatshirt and pants, and went out to the kitchen where I sat in the dark for a few minutes, trying to decide between a nice healthy belt of Scotch or a glass of milk.

A grey shape materialized in the darkness of the kitchen doorway. I lunged for the light switch. When I saw it was Tonia, my pulse dropped about fifty beats.

"Are you all right?" she asked, appearing genuinely concerned.

"Yeah," I said. "I just had a bad dream. Sorry if I woke you up."

She shivered and rubbed her arms. "I couldn't sleep anyhow."

"Well, you could join me in drink," I suggested. "I'm vacillating between Scotch and milk. What's your pleasure?" I got up, walked to the cupboard, and took down two glasses.

"Neither," she said, from behind me.

I turned around in surprise.

"You."

For one of the few times in my life, I was without a clever riposte. I stood there, a glass in each hand, feeling like a tongue-tied adolescent.

"Come to bed with me, Caitlin," she said.

I put the glasses down on the counter behind me, took a deep breath, and looked directly at her. "Tonia," I said, "please don't think I don't want to. God knows I do. But we don't . . . " I shrugged helplessly, "click. We grate. We're like cats and dogs. Oil and water. East and west. We stand for different things. And—"

"For God's sake, Caitlin, I'm not asking you for forever. Just tonight."

She didn't have to ask me again. I stepped toward her and she came eagerly into my arms. Through the thin cotton of her blue pajamas, I could feel her body's warmth as I embraced her. She ran her hands over my shoulders, careful of my bandaged wound, then gripped my arms.

152

"Strong," she commented, surprised.

"We thugs are like that," I said smiling, my lips against her throat.

She laughed, and I felt some of the nervous tension drain out of her.

With my lips I traced the line of her jaw, then brushed her hair aside and began to kiss her ear.

She gasped a little, and I felt her shiver.

Slipping both hands under her pajama top, I caressed the warm length of her back, then the smooth skin over her ribs. When I felt the swell of her breast against my hand, I paused. She made an inarticulate sound and, fitting her body closer to mine, put both hands in my hair, pulled my head back, and kissed me.

I felt as if a jolt of electricity had traveled directly from my lips to somewhere far lower. First I was aware of the exquisite softness of her closed lips, then, as she pressed her mouth to mine, the warm satin wetness of her tongue. It entered between my lips slowly, gently, as if asking permission, then more urgently, meeting mine with an insistence that left no doubt as to what she wanted. Then she withdrew, and I followed, entering her, accepting the invitation of her tongue with my own.

Breathing hard, we finally broke off the kiss. I leaned back against the counter, weak-kneed, my hands on her hips. If some support hadn't been there, I would probably have oozed to the floor. She smiled, and I took her hand. "This is crazy," I said. "Let's go to bed." Fortunately, the spare bedroom was close by.

In the half-light we embraced again, and Tonia's kisses were even fiercer, more urgent this time. So much passion surprised me, but in another moment I understood. This was Tonia's way of holding back the fear. It was a good choice—making love was one of the sweetest distractions I knew.

Tonia peeled me out of my sweatshirt, and I unbuttoned her pajama top and let it fall to the floor. I ran my hands over the incredible softness of her skin, and she shuddered, taking my hands and putting them on her breasts. I felt her nipples harden under my palms, and bent to brush them with my lips. As I took each hard bud in turn in my teeth, Tonia moaned. She put her hands in my hair again, not gently, and raised my head from her breasts. Looking at me for a moment, she kissed me open mouthed, her tongue demanding. I slipped my hands inside her pajama bottoms and held her against me, a knee between her legs, and she began to move against me in a rhythm of her own.

"Caitlin, please," she breathed, taking her mouth from mine.

My hand found her hot, wet center, and she gasped, her arms tightening around me. I stroked her lovely velvet wetness until she began to tremble.

"Now, Caitlin," she gasped, "now."

I slipped inside her and she closed immediately around my fingers in a series of fluttering spasms. As she clung to me and gasped my name, some of the sharp, sweet pleasure that claimed her claimed me, too, and I felt pierced to my soul by the wonder of holding in my hand the throbbing center of her.

I put both my arms around her and held her, stroking her hair and kissing her.

"Come on to bed," I whispered. "Maybe you can stand here all night, but I can't."

"I can't stand at all," she said weakly. "If you weren't holding onto me, I'd collapse."

Getting rid of the last of our clothing, we fell together onto the bed. I pulled the sheets up over us, and she leaned above me on one elbow, looking down. I ran my hands along the long, warm, lovely length of her back, and she sighed.

"Thank you for that," she said.

"You don't need to thank me," I told her, smiling.

She tapped my nose with one finger. "Oh? Is that part of your service, too?"

I chuckled. "Not as a rule. Only under special circumstances."

"Hmmm," she said thoughtfully, bending to kiss me, a little more gently this time.

Through her barely parted lips our tongues met, turning my blood to molten lava, and her tongue invited me to tell her what I needed. For my part, I was fast becoming unable to tolerate much more of this. My desire was now as urgent as hers had been, and I was at the point where it was impossible to delay much longer. As she ran her hands over my breasts, taking my nipples between her fingers, a nova flared in the pit of my stomach. I groaned, and she needed no further invitation. Kissing me once, quickly, she slipped a hand between my thighs, and found the place where I needed to be touched. Her clever fingers opened me like a flower, entering me once, then withdrawing. Beginning a gently, rhythmic stroking, she fanned what was already a red ache of desire to a white hot flame of urgency. I gasped, feeling myself an eager climber approaching the peak of some mountain: almost there, almost there. Then, just when I thought I might faint from desire, a hot wave of liquid gold came boiling down along my nerve endings and swept me away to a place where there was neither sound nor light nor any sensation save the ecstasy that had seized me.

Afterward, in the ebb tide of pleasure, when I could breathe and speak once again, I opened my eyes to find her looking down at me. She brushed my lips with hers, smiled, and smoothed back my sweaty hair.

"Sweet," she said.

Then, settling down beside me, she put her head on my good shoulder. I put one arm around her, and was about to say something — nothing important — but when I looked down, she was asleep.

I lay there in the dark for a long time until I was certain she was deeply asleep. Then, very gently, I wriggled out from under her sleeping weight. She murmured once, then turned over, sighing. I tucked the blankets around her, put my sweatshirt and pants back on, and left her, closing the door quietly behind me.

In the gloom of the hallway, I paused for one moment, tempted to go back to that bed, pull the blankets over Tonia and me, fit my body to hers, and join her in oblivion. But I couldn't. Quite apart from the bonding I feared might happen if Tonia lay in my arms all night, there was the job ahead of me. I needed my mind clear for it. Afterwards? Well, we'd see.

* * * * *

I got a beer from the kitchen, and took it into my bedroom with me. As I lay there drinking, getting sleepier by the minute, I found my thoughts turning away from Tonia, back to the dream I had had earlier.

Funny. I hadn't thought about Aunt Fee for years, let alone dreamed of the Dark Lady. Well, maybe my reading of Shakespeare's Dark Lady sonnet had caused Aunt Fee's *bête noir* to stir in my id. They weren't the same creature, of course. Still, my subconscious had made a connection between them. What did it mean?

Was this another facet of the Llewelyn prescience? I shook my head. If so, it was worse than the bloody Delphic oracle. It was far too indirect for me. Since I hadn't heard a peep from this particular province of my subconscious for years, why was it trying to communicate now? I yawned, and decided to ignore the dream. To hell with it. Everyone was entitled to bad dreams now and then, right?

I wrapped myself in my bedclothes and let myself fall back into the oily pool of sleep. As I submerged, I thought I sensed an insistent voice yammering at me from a distant place.

156

Something seemed to be scratching urgently at the door of my mind, begging to be let in, but I was far too tired to listen. I had one single sharp, bright thought, but it slipped through my tired mind like a firefly, and the rising tide of sleep soon snuffed it out.

SATURDAY

Chapter 14

A shroud of fog lay over the city Saturday morning, and it didn't seem to be the kind that had come in on little cat feet. It looked solid and serious. Had I tried, I couldn't have designed a more Gothic setting for the end of this sordid little tale of blackmail.

The phone rang. It was Gray.

"I received your message last night," she explained in her flawless English. "However, it was too late to call."

"I may need your help," I told her. "Later tonight I'll be speaking with a gentleman I don't know very well. He's the physical type, I think. I would appreciate having the girls on hand to dissuade him from getting physical with me."

"I understand," Gray said. Then, after a pause: "Should I accompany them?"

Animals weren't the only critters with whom Gray could communicate. Was my lack of self confidence so apparent? I wasn't insulted, though. Far from it. I'd take all the help I could get. "That might be a good idea," I said. "I'll need to contact you with the time and place." Damn! There was no phone at the farmhouse. "Gray, when are you going to persuade your aunt to get a phone? Or maybe I should try."

"It's not my place to try to persuade her of anything," Gray said. "She brought us out of Vietnam on a leaky thirteen-foot fishing boat and saved us from rape and murder by pirates. What advice could you or I possible give such a woman?"

I felt ashamed. Gray was right. It was none of my business.

"However," she said, "I will be in the flower packing barn all afternoon. You may call me there."

"Thanks, Gray."

"You're welcome," she said formally, and hung up.

I began to feel more confident. My plans, such as they were, were starting to fall into place.

I found Tonia in jeans and a white sweatshirt, tossing old coffee grounds down the drain, and resisting Repo's blandishments. I let her make coffee while I fed the starving cat, then we sat across the table from each other. She smiled at me once—a secret smile—then looked away. I felt a surge of relief. So she, too, felt that there was no need to refer to what had happened last night. But as I looked at her, I also felt one sharp twinge of regret. Might-have-beens are always poignant.

"You seem awfully cool," she said, raising an eyebrow. "Today's the day, you know."

"Today's the day all right," I agreed. "Cool? Well, why not—it's almost over. Right?"

She looked at me with a little more confidence than she had the other day. Not much, but a little. I tried not to preen.

162

"Didn't Farkas say he'd call about noon?" she asked.

I checked my watch. It wasn't yet nine. Should I let her chew her cuticles for three hours, or should I gamble and tell her what I had planned? I decided to compromise. "Relax," I told her, exaggerating my optimism about sixty-five percent. "I've got it all under control."

She raised a skeptical eyebrow again. She did that sort of thing rather well. I guess it intimidated the hell out of the undergraduates. But by now I'd seen it too often. When I didn't begin to tremble and ask for the equivalent of an extension on my term paper, she resorted to speech. "Oh?",

The heat of the night before seemed to recede a bit further as I poured a mug of coffee and nodded sagely. "I'd rather not discuss the details," I told her. "You might inadvertently communicate a hint to Farkas over the phone—you know, sound just a little bit too feisty. Make him suspect that something's up." I wanted badly to tell her that I'd found the letters and that they were safe, but I couldn't realistically trust her. If Farkas started gloating over the phone, she'd probably forget herself and tell him to go to hell. Which wouldn't be a bad place for him. But I needed to do it my way. I wanted Mr. Farkas to tell me a few things.

"But something *is* up, isn't it?"

I nodded wisely again. "Cross my heart." I thought it would be tempting fate to add the latter part of that oath.

She shook her head in disappointment. "I guess I've got to go on trusting you."

"Seems silly to stop now," I remarked. "Besides, unless you want to call in the police, or pay the blackmail money, what other option do you have?"

"None," she said, the old pain-in-the-butt Tonia resurfacing.

"Tonia, it's going to be all right," I said, attempting to reassure her. "I know you don't have much confidence in me, but this *isn't* the first time I've done something like this."

She poured herself a cup of coffee and started for the study. "I'm trying to remember that," she said. "I'm sorry. I'm just . . . frightened."

"I know," I commiserated. "Listen, I have to go meet someone in a few minutes," I told her. "But I'll be back in plenty of time to coach you for the phone call. And to get you over to your place to receive it."

She began to say something, thought better of it, then shrugged and nodded. Turning her back on me, she headed for the study.

Repo looked at me quizzically.

"Beats me," I said to him. "Anyone would think she had no faith in me."

He began to furiously wash a back leg.

"Another Doubting Thomas I don't need," I informed him. "Go sharpen your claws on the apple tree. Although you hardly need it — you've wounded me to the quick."

* * * * *

I was glad to see that Lester was punctual. It meant he was taking things seriously. Right on the dot of ten he came through the door of British Fish 'N Chips, a large brown envelope in his hand. He looked a trifle haggard, I noted. Well, I hoped he was learning that a life of crime was not as cushy as that of a journalism student.

"I got them," he said with a weak smile, pushing the envelope across the table to me.

I ordered coffee for both of us, and then opened the envelope and looked inside. He seemed to have kept his word. As nearly as I could tell, there were photos of all the electronic goods I had seen in the house on Redfern. Backs, fronts, and serial numbers.

"Are your buddies ready to work tonight?" I asked him.

164

He grimaced. "They thought I was joking. It took me a long time to persuade them I wasn't." He licked his lips nervously. "But they don't want to go to jail any more than I do. So they'll do it. I mean we'll do it." He raised his eyebrows in alarm. "Unless you have something else you want me to do. Instead, that is."

I would never have thought of it had Lester not volunteered his services. The idea just popped into my head. "Lester, is there a lens or something that lets you shoot pictures at night?"

He nodded. "Sure. It's the equivalent of a starlight scope. Same technology. It takes available light—starlight, moonlight—and magnifies it eighty thousand times. Makes even the darkest scene pretty bright. I don't have one, though."

"Can you rent one?"

"I suppose so. The camera shop where I do business has a couple."

I thought this over again. It seemed like a terrific idea. Insurance usually is. "I may want you to take some pictures tonight. Go rent the scope." I took out my wallet and peeled off a couple of fifties. "That should be enough. Just make sure you stick around today so I can tell you where this little assignment will be, and exactly what sort of pictures I want."

He nodded, then could not prevent himself from yawning. "I'll be waiting to hear from you. Right now I'm going to go home and sleep. After I rent the scope, that is." He swallowed the last of his coffee and looked at me curiously. "Can I ask you something."

"Sure. Shoot."

"What do I call you? Can you tell me your first name, at least?"

I didn't see why not. "It's Caitlin," I said.

He got up from the table and stood there for a moment, looking gangly and awkward. I felt a surge of affection for him. "Caitlin," he asked, "will this assignment tonight be ... dangerous?"

"Maybe for me," I told him. "But not for you. You just do what I tell you and no one will even know you're there."

"You're going to meet Farkas, aren't you? By yourself."

I nodded, deciding to save the girls and Gray for a surprise. Just in case my amateur photographer happened to turn his coat.

He swallowed nervously. "Be careful with that guy. I've seen him lift Harrington and Jerome right off the floor—one hanging on each of his arms." He shivered.

"Thanks for the warning," I told him. "I'll keep it in mind. Now go get the scope and have a nice nap. We have work to do tonight."

Chapter 15

I picked Tonia up at eleven and we drove through the fog to her condominium. The stately Gary Oaks towered over us, ghostly shapes that disappeared drippingly into the mist, underscoring my sense of the unreal. Perhaps this *was* just a bad dream, I thought, one from which I would soon awaken. I doubted it though. I didn't often have an itching, half-healed bullet wound in my dreams. Or a case of high anxiety.

Inside, I pulled the drapes and turned on all the living room lights. Tonia went to the kitchen to make coffee and I followed her, closing and latching the shutters. If she thought me a little paranoid, she said nothing. Perhaps a week of incarceration with me had accustomed her to the bizarre. Well, her parole was at hand. As soon as Farkas was neutralized, she could move back in here. By now I looked forward to the event as much as I believed she did.

I attached my earphone and recorder to the telephone and we sat there and looked at each other.

"Just tell him what he wants to hear," I told her.

"And that is?" she inquired.

I sighed. Good old testy Tonia. "That you're scared to death, that you'll meet him anywhere, and that you've got the money." She looked a little alarmed, and I tried to reassure her. "Remember, you're not paying. And you're not going anywhere—I am."

She snorted. "Scum," she said.

Speak of the devil. As if on cue, the phone rang. I started the recorder, and motioned for Tonia to pick up the phone. I took the dining room extension.

"Hi there," a cheery voice said. It was the same voice we had heard on Monday. Then, I had assumed it belonged to a much younger man. Now, I was sure it was Farkas' voice. He wouldn't want to deprive himself of the pleasure of hearing his victim squirm. "You've got the money, I presume."

"I've got it," Tonia replied coolly.

"Good girl, good girl," Farkas intoned as if he were talking to a dog. "Listen up and I'll tell you where to bring it."

"I'm listening."

"As you drive along the ocean on Dallas Road, you'll come to an observation point. I'm sure you know it—Clover Point."

"I know it."

"All right. Be there at nine tonight. Park your car and blink your headlights three times. You'll see a light flash twice down in the rocks. Throw the money in the direction of the light. Then get back in your car and wait."

"I want to know when I get the first letter," Tonia said.

"Don't interrupt," the voice replied. "As soon as I see the money, I'll decide if it's a sufficiently large goodwill gesture."

168

"You bastard!" Tonia exploded. "You said—"

"Don't interrupt me!" Farkas shouted. "You bloody interfering woman! Make me any angrier and I'll have to really punish you. It will make what you've gone through so far look like a picnic."

Sounds of heavy breathing came across the line, and I motioned for Tonia to control herself. If the situation hadn't been so serious, I might have laughed out loud. I wonder if Farkas knew how ridiculous he sounded. I guessed not.

"I've said all I intend to," he told her. "You have your instructions. When you start receiving the letters will depend on my mood. We're going to have many conversations, you and I. Don't make me angry, Dr. Dyke. Never make me angry."

Tonia listened to this drivel with lips tightly pressed together. But she seemed to be under control. "Is that all?" she asked Farkas.

"That's it," he told her. "Until nine tonight."

She hung up.

We sat in silence for a few minutes.

"I've never hated anyone before," she said at last. "But I hate that man." She took a deep breath. "Caitlin," she confessed, "I'm about at the end of my emotional resources with this thing. I expected to get some support from Val, but she hasn't even called. I know it's foolish of me, but I'd appreciate hearing just how you know everything will be all right." She blinked her eyes rapidly, and I could tell she was about to cry.

"Okay," I said reluctantly. "I'll tell you. But not here. Let's go have some lunch."

* * * * *

Over salmon sandwiches and apple crisp at Burt's I told her as much of the story, and my plans, as I wanted her to

169

know. Basically that I had the letters, that I would be getting some help tonight, and that I had a plan to neutralize Farkas for good.

"I can't believe that you just . . . *do* these things! Break into people's offices and homes. Rifle through their belongings. Aren't you ever afraid you'll be caught?"

I shrugged, a little surprised that she was still hung up on this aspect of my activities. "Well, I try to minimize that likelihood. But yes, I do worry about it."

"God, Caitlin, you take such chances."

I made an equivocal sound as I thought this over. I've never been a risk taker. I don't have a T-type personality. I'm really very careful. Chances? I didn't think so.

Tonia said accusingly, "Why didn't you tell me this before?"

"Because I didn't want you to let Farkas know."

"Why not?" she demanded angrily. "If he knew you have the letters, then you wouldn't have to go and meet him. We could have concluded this over the phone."

"I don't think so," I told her. "Farkas isn't just going to lick his wounds and go away. He's going to need some persuading."

"Why? What could he possibly do now that you have the letters? And what could you do to him anyhow?"

I shrugged, reluctant to tell her about my bad feelings about Farkas. She'd probably laugh. But damn it anyway, I knew this wasn't as simple as it seemed. What could I tell her—that in my Llewelyn genes I had an unshakable feeling of some revelation impending? No, that would only alarm her all over again. Better to have her believe that Farkas simply needed to be thoroughly stomped on before he would let go of this particular bone. Who care if she continued to think I was a thug?

"I don't think he'll give up with out a fight," I said. While true, it was not, of course, the whole truth. But what was? I had a terrible feeling that I was only hours from finding out.

"And you're just dying to be the one who makes him cry uncle, aren't you? Damn it, Caitlin, I don't see why you have to drag this out! Meeting him is bound to be dangerous. Or is that what you want?"

"What?"

"The shootout at the O.K. Corral. Caitlin Reece dispensing justice with her .357. Is that why you're so reluctant to let this thing with Farkas go?" She raked her hair a few times, obviously warming up for a long harangue. I decided it was time to leave. I needed time to find a white hat for the shootout.

* * * * *

She marched into the house and barricaded herself in the study, obviously figuring that further association with me might be dangerous to her moral health. I went into my bedroom and got out my gun cleaning kit, took it and my .357 Magnum into the living room, put Purcell's *Dido and Aeneas* on the stereo, and went to work. In an hour or so I was satisfied with the condition of my firearm. Although I didn't intend to use it, I wanted no surprises. I loaded it with brand new .357 factory ammunition—full wadcutter load this time: it makes a bigger hole—and slipped two speed loaders into my pocket. I poured myself a large Perrier with lots of ice, and settled down to make my phone calls.

Lester sounded nervous but ready. He assured me he had the scope. I told him I'd pick him up at the British Fish 'N Chips at eight tonight. I suggested he wear dark clothing. Something warm.

Gray sounded the same as she always did. We could have been discussing the latest shipment of daffodils to Ottawa. I told her where I was meeting Farkas and when, and she assured me she'd be there in advance. We rehearsed the signals that would bring the girls to me, and I assured her I still had my dog whistle. I reviewed the sequence of signals that would send the girls back to her. She sound a little puzzled, so I explained things—if I really did get in a shootout with Farkas, I wanted the girls well out of danger. Their purpose, after all, was only window dressing. Gray understood.

I called Francis' number, and to my intense frustration, it was still busy. I briefly considered going over there and kicking in his door. Oh well, I rationalized, if he had dug up anything really important about Buchanan, he'd have called me.

Then there was nothing else to do except change clothes and wait. I put on my favorite old jeans, navy sneakers and socks, and a heavy black wool turtleneck. I put my .357, my dark windbreaker, and a pair of gloves on the bed beside me. Then I closed my eyes and tried to compose my thoughts. I had a little over three hours to wait.

Farkas. I wasn't worried that he'd discover the letters were gone. I believed, as Lester had intimated, that he never intended to give them back. I'm sure he anticipated many phone calls in which he humiliated Tonia, holding out hope, promising next time, next time, and never delivering. But why? My mind pursued that question again and again until it felt like a hamster on a wheel. Give it up, Caitlin, I told myself.

But the feeling of something approaching, something shuffling through the darkness like a mute, hulking beast, would not leave me. It's nothing, I told myself. Just my own fear. A perfectly normal thing. Dismiss it. I decided to try to sleep. I took four more aspirin, set my alarm for seven-thirty, closed my eyes, and emptied my mind.

It seemed only minutes later that the alarm went off. I reached over and silenced it. Then it was time to go. Tonia's door, I noted, was firmly closed. Like her mind. Ah well, I thought, we thugs don't need coddling. Not much, anyhow.

Chapter 16

Lester didn't want anything to eat. Neither did I. We ordered coffee, and toyed with the cups.

"You're so calm," he observed.

"A cunning pose," I told him. "Actually, I'm a nervous wreck."

"So why do you do these things?" he asked.

I debated giving him another smart answer, then decided the truth might do as well. "Because they have to be done," I said, "and I'm able to do them." The words surprised even me. I had never said them to anyone before. Why him, why now? I wasn't sure. I had begun to feel very mortal in the past few hours. Perhaps I wanted to be remembered as more than a thug.

He took off his glasses, polished them furiously on a napkin, and finally met my eyes. "Oh," he said.

Briefly, I explained what I wanted him to do.

"Is that all?" he asked, sounding disappointed.

"It's enough," I said. "Keep out of sight, and keep looking through the scope. Make sure you get pictures of me and Farkas. Especially if he tries any funny business. No matter what happens, don't you dare make a sound. And if I'm, ah . . . in no shape to collect the film from you at the end of the evening, call this man." I wrote Sandy's name and number on a matchbook and gave it to Lester. "He's with the Oak Bay Police Department. Give him the film and the negatives of the stolen property. Tell him the whole story—at least as much of it as you know."

Lester stared into his coffee cup.

"Lester," I said softly. "Don't go all wimpy on me now. I need you."

He looked up, swallowing manfully. "All right."

"What about Harrington and Jerome?" I asked. "Are they ready to go to work?"

Lester nodded. "They've got two delivery companies lined up. The stuff should be returned by ten or so. They're going to move their belongings out in the meantime. We've rented a new place. Farkas doesn't know about it."

"Okay. Let's go, Lester. Showtime."

He gave me a tremulous smile. I linked my arm through his and we went out to slay the dragon.

* * * * *

Fog-shrouded Clover Point looked like a set from *The Hound of the Baskervilles*, lacking only a little canine baying. I wondered if the girls would oblige. Actually, I was surprised that visibility was as good as it was. The sodium vapor lights in the parking lot were a great help. I found a spot for Lester on

176

the grassy verge of the embankment, behind a cluster of garbage containers. It was just after nine, but I wanted Lester in place before either Farkas or Gray arrived. I drove back onto Dallas Road and parked on the street, just across from the point. Then I settled down in my car to wait.

Farkas showed up at nine forty-five. He drove the Buick wagon onto the point, parked, and got out. Then I lost sight of him. I guessed he was going to secrete himself in the rocks, whence he intended to pop up like an evil gnome, scaring Tonia witless. Except he didn't have Tonia to contend with—he had me.

I drove my MG onto the point and took a space several yards away from Farkas' car. I blinked my headlights three times. Almost at once an answering pair of blinks came from the rocks on my right. I turned off the MG's engine, reached behind the seat, and took an old backpack off the floor. Earlier I had stuffed it with a bunch of newspaper cut to the same size as currency, and bound with a rubber band. Farkas was about to get a surprise. I slammed the car door, put the dog whistle to my lips, and blew two short and two long blasts, inaudible to me. I will admit that I prayed a little, too.

They came loping out of the fog, those wonderful, enormous, brindled hounds, and I let them smell my hands, then hugged them. The cavalry had arrived. They took up positions one on each side of me, and I felt suddenly hopeful. I heaved the backpack down into the rocks with a fillip of savage glee. Then I unholstered my gun, held it down by my side, finger on the trigger guard, and waited. The girls waited beside me, silent and patient. Farkas didn't make us wait long.

A gargle of muffled rage came out of the fog, and I felt a sharp, shameful spasm of satisfaction. The girls moved a little, uneasily. Then, from the embankment came a noisy scrabbling, and suddenly Farkas loomed out of the fog. He took several steps toward me, and I decided he had come close enough.

"Stay right there," I told him.

He turned his flashlight on and shone it in my face. I closed my eyes to preserve my night vision and held my .357 Magnum out in plain sight, muzzle pointed at the sky. "Shut that light off, or I'll shoot it out."

The light was dutifully extinguished. "You're not Tonia Konig," he said. "So who are you?" The voice was harsh, imperious.

I blinked a few times, and my vision returned to normal. I could see him only as a dark, featureless shape outlined against the fog. I hoped Lester's scope was working better than my eyes. "I'm just a friend," I told him. "A kind of advisor. Tonight, though, I'm a messenger."

He laughed. "Well, messenger, your friend owes me some money. And I didn't find your little joke with the backpack very amusing. You know," he told me, "I think I might add an extra thousand to my bill for that piece of foolishness. You can tell that to Dr. Konig. But first, I want the money she was to deliver tonight."

"Oh, really?" I said. "Well, you have something of hers, too. Why don't you let me see it. Then maybe we can talk money."

He laughed unpleasantly. "I must have forgotten to bring it."

I knew it! He hadn't even checked on the letters. While he was still cocky, believing himself to have the upper hand, maybe I could trick him into divulging a few pieces of information.

Farkas continued, "But if I got the money, say right now, I could always mail the letter to her."

My antennae started to vibrate—why did Farkas always speak about "her," and not "them?"

"On second thought, maybe I'll mail it to the newspaper," Farkas threatened. "Or the university. You know, I said I'd do that if she didn't follow my instructions." He was warming to the subject now, and I wanted to keep him talking.

"Well, maybe you'll have to do that," I said. "We've been wondering if keeping this thing quiet is worth it. This is one hell of a lot of money to fork over on trust. We have only your word that you'll keep your mouth shut. Maybe once you get the money you'll spill the beans anyhow."

Come on, Farkas, I muttered impatiently to myself. Give! Tell me what's in this for you. Besides the money.

He chuckled.

"We've been talking things over this week," I improvised. "We've almost decided you're asking too much."

It worked. "You've come here to *bargain*?" he said incredulously. "You don't have anything to bargain *with*!" He laughed unpleasantly. The girls growled, a menacing throaty duet.

"Sure we do," I told him.

"Oh?" he asked. "What?"

I was fed up with this fencing. Maybe the shock of hearing the facts would loosen his tongue. "Have you checked the bottom drawer of your office filing cabinet lately?"

Farkas stood absolutely still for a moment while the words penetrated. "No!" he howled, and took a few running steps toward me. Warning growls from the girls brought him up short—I'd not yet met the person who would charge two growling Great Danes. I could see his face pretty clearly now, and it wasn't a pleasant sight. "You little bitch," he said, opening and closing his fists. I was pretty sure what he wanted to close them around.

Now it was my turn to do some crowing. I had to make him sufficiently angry to be heedless of what he said. "You blew it, Farkas," I taunted him. "Beaten by a bunch of women."

He panted and snorted a little, but said nothing.

"Now what, Victor? Are you going to send James Harrington to run Tonia down in the park again? Or shoot at her in her study? Or hang around her back yard and spy on her?" I decided I might as well help Lester out, too. "Or maybe you'll get the resident photographer to take some more candid shots."

Silence. By now I was seething. Damn it, Farkas, talk!

"Forget it, friend. It's all over. I've beaten you. I've got the letters, your extortion notes, and the two phone calls you made to Tonia. That seems like a lot of years in prison to me. And if you're thinking of falling back on the burglary scam, you can forget that, too. Your young accomplices have suddenly seen the error of their ways. In fact, right about now they're returning the stolen goods. You're alone, Victor. It's finished."

I let this sink in for a minute, before throwing him a bone. "Of course," I added, as if the thought had only then occurred to me, "I don't *have* to hand you over to the police."

"Oh?" he asked, a sly tone coming into his voice. "Why not? What do you want?"

"Not much," I told him. "I just want you to stay away from Tonia Konig. Far away. I'm going to keep the letters and photos and tapes in a safe place, and if I hear that she's so much as sprained an ankle getting out of bed, I'm going to assume it was your doing."

He thought this over for a minute. "What else?"

"You're to stay away from Valerie Frazier, too. I don't want to have to worry about you harassing her. So the same rules apply to her as to Tonia. This thing is *over*, Victor."

Then he did something that completely surprised me—he threw back his head and laughed. Loudly and long. Fool that I was, I attached no particular meaning to it, apart from Farkas' own brand of nuttiness.

But I still didn't have my answer. Why *had* he been persecuting Tonia? Well, it didn't look as though I would get it. I just couldn't make him talk. I had underestimated him—he wasn't what I had expected. He might be an addle-brained misogynist, but he wasn't a wild-eyed maniac. In fact, he seemed rather clever to me. And cool. Maybe too cool for a man whose future was at stake. Damn it all, what did he know that I didn't? I suddenly decided I had nothing to lose by asking.

"Why have you been trying to scare Tonia Konig half to death?" The next thought just popped into my head and out my mouth before I had a chance to censor it: "Is someone holding your leash, Victor?"

There was no laughter this time. Had I hit the nail on the head? I was so surprised that I didn't notice him moving backwards toward the edge of the embankment. Abruptly he turned and . . . disappeared. In a moment, the fog had swallowed him.

"Shit!" I yelled, running to the cliff edge and looking over. The fog made it impossible to see more than what was directly below me. I didn't dare follow him or send the girls. I heard sounds of clumsy flight, a body falling heavily onto the rocks below, and a series of splashes. Then, nothing. "Farkas!" I shouted. Damn it anyway, had he fallen over the edge and broken his neck?

When Gray appeared beside me, a dark shape in black windbreaker and jeans, I thought my heart might stop. She snapped her fingers, and the girls flanked her. "The man you call Farkas has gone," she told me.

"Gone? Then he's all right?"

"Apparently. He fled along the rocks. He will probably climb the embankment closer to town, wait awhile, then come back here for his car."

"Damn!" I swore.

"Why reproach yourself?" Gray asked me shrugging. "You told him the conditions under which he could remain free. What reasonable man would ignore them?"

What reasonable man, indeed?

* * * * *

The evening had an unfinished feel about it, like an interrupted conversation. Well, what was I to do—wait for Farkas on Clover Point, hoping he'd return for his car? Or go back to Redfern Street and beard him in his den? And then what? Beat on him? Demand to know what I was certain he was hiding from me? With a sigh, I decided to let it go. Farkas had run away, intimidated by my ferocious self. End of story.

I dropped Lester off at his new digs — a duplex on Fernwood Street. Not very prepossessing, but at least it was safe.

"Looks like the guys aren't back yet," Lester said. "Funny, I thought they'd have finished long ago. Oh well, maybe they're still getting their stuff from the old house. Or drinking. I could use a few beers myself."

I guessed that was an invitation, and decided to decline. "You'd probably be better off with a good night's sleep," I suggested in a motherly fashion. "By the way, it's a moot point now, but how do you think the pictures will turn out?"

"Real good," he said, patting his camera. "But I'm sure glad you won't need them."

"Well, that's what you buy insurance for," I said tritely.

"And those dogs — they were terrific," he said appreciatively. "So were you, come to think of it. God, I'm surprised Farkas stood there and took all that from you." He yawned. "What happens now, Caitlin?"

"Beats me," I admitted. "If he stays away from Dr. Konig and from Valerie Frazier, he has nothing to worry about."

Lester nodded. "Say, what did you mean about someone holding his leash? Do you really think someone else made him harass Dr. Konig?"

I shrugged. "Maybe I like to make things more complex than they are."

"Well . . . " Lester said.

"Goodnight, kiddo," I told him fondly. "You were terrific, too. I appreciate your help."

"Um, listen Caitlin," he said, "if you ever, you know, need me to help you again . . . "

"I know where to find you," I assured him. "Now go get some sleep."

* * * * *

The house was dark when I got back. I was surprised. Not that I expected a homecoming party, but a smidgen of interest in how the proceedings had gone would not have been unwelcome. Thinking I should at least offer to recount the night's events, I tapped on Tonia's door, and called softly.

Belatedly, I saw the note: *I can't stand this, Caitlin. I've gone to bed with your bottle of Scotch. Talk to you in the morning.*

Oh, to hell with it, I thought. Maybe Repo would be interested.

From the phone in the kitchen I made yet another call to Francis. This time his phone rang and rang. No answer. I hung up the receiver thoughtfully. The ferret was apparently not at home—about as unlikely an occurrence as snow in August. I shrugged. He was already hours late with my information—or unable to find any. I yawned. Well, Valerie would have to extricate herself from Buchanan's clutches without my help. As for the tardy ferret, I decided I'd pay him a visit early next week and eloquently request a refund on my five hundred dollar advance.

I took a hot shower, poured myself an enormous cognac, and climbed into bed. Repo joined me, and I began telling him the story of the fleeing extortionist. He might have been willing to listen to the entire sorry tale—I don't know. Suddenly the alcohol, my fatigue, and the night's events juggernauted over me, and I was scarcely able to turn off the light before I was asleep.

SUNDAY

Chapter 17

How long had the phone been ringing? I fumbled for it, knocking over my alarm clock and a glass of water in the process. "What?" I croaked.

This hiss of long distance preceded Francis' voice. "You are *so* hard to get hold of!" he complained.

I swung my legs out of bed and sat up. "You should talk, you reneging little piranha! Talk to me, Francis."

"Don't be so mean to me, Caitlin," he pouted. "When I tell you what I've done for you in the past twenty-four hours, you'll probably kiss me."

"Don't count on it, buster. Come on, Francis, let's have it."

I could hear him take a deep breath. "I'm at some sleazy motel on the mainland," he said, "and I've had to spend a lot of money—most of it mine, I might add—but I've got what you want on Buchanan." I sat up straight, my heartbeat accelerating. "There was a well-buried police report which is very interesting indeed. Apparently Baxter Carlisle Buchanan was a very naughty boy thirty-one years ago."

The suspense was making me crazy. "The bottom line, Francis."

He sniffed. "You emotional women—so impatient! You want the bottom line—okay here it is. Thirty-one years ago, Buchanan murdered his first wife. And got away with it. At least that's my reading of things. It seems she was cheating on him—or he thought she was cheating on him—and he shot her. The official story, for your information, is that she was shot by an intruder, but the facts on the police report don't suggest that. There was more than enough evidence to bring him to trial, but the Buchanans are pretty influential in this part of the country. And his wife was just a poor kid from up north somewhere. His family never wanted him to marry her anyway, but it seems he really loved her—he went crazy when he suspected that she had been doing things behind his back. So the whole affair was hushed up. For thirty-one years."

By this time I was on my feet, all my alarms going off. "Jesus Christ, Francis—did you just find this out? If you've been holding out on me—"

"Caitlin, relax! You have my word. I just got the report an hour and a half ago. I phoned you right away. Why the hell don't you have an answering machine? I've been calling you on and off since Saturday morning with my suspicions, but I had no real hard information until now."

"Okay, Francis. I'm sorry. It's just that this is . . . dynamite. Is there anything else I should know right now?"

"I don't think so," he said. "You can come by and pick up the report tomorrow."

"Right." I started shedding sweatpants and shirt, fumbling around in the dark for my clothes. "I have to run, Francis. Thanks. Bye."

So Buchanan had been so crazy with jealousy that he had killed his first wife, had he? I shivered. Zipping my jeans and ramming my feet into my Nikes, I had my hand on the telephone to call Valerie when it rang under my palm, scaring me witless.

"Yes!" I yelled into the receiver.

A horrible gaspy wheezing was my only reply. I was about to hang up, thinking this a new variation on the obscene phone call, when a tiny voice moaned, "*Caitlinnn . . .*"

"Who's this?" I answered.

"Uhhh . . . uhhh . . . " the voice said.

I realized that whoever was calling me was weeping uncontrollably. "Who *is* this?" I shouted.

"Mmmmm . . . me. It's me—Lester," the voice stuttered. I realized then that the voice also sounded scared to death.

"Lester? For God's sake, it's three a.m. What the hell's the matter?"

He blubbered for a few moments, then managed to squeeze out a few coherent words. "They're dead, Caitlin. Oh God. All of them. Dead."

My mouth suddenly dry, I asked the question. "Who, Lester? Who's dead?"

"*All* of them!" he shrieked as if addressing a moron. "Harrington, Jerome . . . and Farkas, too."

My mind was a complete blank. Perhaps I was having a nightmare. Or maybe Lester was. "How do you know this, Lester?"

"Because I'm right here with them. In the house on Redfern Street. They've been shot . . . there's blood everywhere. Oh God, Caitlin. What should I do?"

"Get the hell out of there," I told him.

"I can't. I'm afraid," he stuttered. "Maybe whoever did this is looking for me, too."

"All the more reason to get out." I tried to visualize the house on Redfern. Wasn't there a low fence in the back yard, and an alley separating it from the next street? I thought so. "Go out the back door and down the alley. I'll meet you on the corner of the next street over."

"Caitlin, I can't!"

"You bloody well better manage it, buster, Hide in the bushes or something. I'll be on the corner in ten minutes." I hung up.

It took me about fifteen additional seconds to pull my sweater on and grab my windbreaker. I checked the .357 and patted my pockets to make sure the speed loaders were still in place. Should I take time to call Valerie? I couldn't decide. And what about Sandy? Things were very quickly becoming unravelled, and I sure could use a little help. But first, I had to take care of Lester.

* * * * *

He bolted from a stand of rhododendron bushes like a hunted stag, yanked open the car door, and collapsed on the passenger seat. Covering his face with his hands, he moaned a little. I shoved a half-full bottle of cognac at him.

"Take a drink, Lester. A big one. And calm down."

While Lester drank, I drove. I found a Seven-Eleven with a well-lit parking lot, and turned in. He handed the bottle back to me and I took a swig myself. Couldn't hurt, I reasoned.

"What were you dong back at that house, damn it?" I demanded.

He took a deep breath. "Harrington and Jerome didn't come back. I called the people at the delivery services, then all our friends. Then I started to think maybe something awful had happened to them." He sniffled a little. "The worst thing I could think of was Harrington decided to go back and try to patch things up with Farkas, and Farkas had beaten the shit out of them. So I went to check it out. I was going to sneak in the back door but it was open when I got there. And there they were. All three of them. In the living room. Shot in the head." He started to shake again. "It didn't look like Farkas had been beating on anyone, but I couldn't be sure. I kind of freaked out, I guess. Took the phone and called you from the front hall closet."

Smart kid—when in doubt, retreat into the closet. "Did you see anyone, Lester?"

He shook his head.

"Think! Anyone on the street? A car that didn't belong there? Someone driving away?"

He shook his head again, then turned to look at me. "Caitlin, I just don't remember. Maybe there was a big black car, but maybe not. I'm a little mixed up right now."

"Maybe you're not," I told him. "Think about that big black car. Try to *see* it."

He dutifully closed his eyes.

"What can you tell me about it?"

"Shiny," he said. "Long. Foreign. A Jaguar," he said with conviction. "I remember the hood ornament."

It was too much to hope for, but I had to know. "How about the driver? Did you get a look at him?"

He opened his eyes. "No. That's all I can tell you. Just the stuff about the car. Sorry."

I let out the breath I had been holding. What I didn't want to tell Lester was that if he had seen the car, in all probability the driver had seen him. And I had a pretty good idea who the driver was.

"Do you think the guy in the Jag was . . . " he swallowed audibly, "the killer?"

"Yeah," I said, "I do."

He hunched down in the seat, trying to disappear. Well, I couldn't help him vanish, but I could arrange the next best thing. I could add him to my collection of orphans of the storm.

"How would you like to come home with me?" I said brightly. "Malcolm and Yvonne—the people upstairs from me—won't be home tonight. You'll have to seep on their couch with the cat, but if you don't mind, he probably won't."

That coaxed a wan smile from him. "Okay," he said. "Thanks, Caitlin."

* * * * *

I took Lester up the outside stairs and used the key Yvonne keeps in the begonia pot to let him in. I stayed just long enough to tell him where to find the bathroom and some blankets, and hurried back downstairs to my place. I was beginning to have a terrible feeling about all this.

I hammered on Tonia's door loudly enough to wake the dead, then barged in and turned on the light. "Get up and throw some clothes on," I told her.

"What?" she mumbled sleepily from her nest of blankets.

"Get up damn it! And hurry up about it."

For once she didn't give me any back talk. She put her clothes on over her pajamas, and when she had pulled her sweater over her head, I tossed the key to Malcolm and Yvonne's apartment at her.

"Go on upstairs and lock yourself in," I ordered.

"Why—" she started.

"I don't have time to explain," I told her. "Please, Tonia, just do it. There's a badly frightened kid up there—maybe you can help soothe him. But don't put the lights on and don't tromp around. I want the place to seem empty if . . . " I trailed off.

"If what?" she demanded.

"If someone comes looking for me. Now go on and do what I told you. And if you have to, call the police."

She looked appropriately frightened. "What happened tonight, Caitlin? It all went wrong, didn't it?"

Ah, such confidence. I shook my head and pointed to the door. "Later. Just go upstairs."

She opened her mouth to ask another question, but after a look at my face, changed her mind. I heard the door close, the sounds of her feet on the outside stairs, then the creaking of floorboards overhead. A murmur of voices. Then, nothing.

I dialed Valerie's number. It rang eighteen times before I gave up. Letting the door to my house slam shut behind me, I raced outside to my MG. I knew who I was after now. I just didn't know where to find him.

As I drove down deserted Oak Bay Avenue, I cursed my stupidity. I had been on a parallel path to the truth from the beginning. Damn it anyway—I'd *known* Farkas hadn't been harboring some nutty misogynistic urge. It had just *felt* wrong. Why hadn't I paid attention to my intuition? I shook my head. Because I'd been afraid to. Because I had wanted to reason my way to the truth. The analytical sleuth, solving the riddle by the cold clear light of logic. Not the frowzy tealeaf reader, Madame Caitlin, coaxing the truth out of a dark pattern in a cracked cup.

No, I had held the truth in my hands the afternoon I'd ransacked Farkas' trunk and found his old Air Force pictures. But I had ignored it. A coincidence, I'd told myself. Oh, sure. Some coincidence—Baxter Buchanan's wife being blackmailed by Victor Farkas. The fact that Farkas just happened to be an old Air Force buddy of Buchanan's and kept a scrapbook full of newspaper clippings of Buchanan's exploits was, of course, unrelated. What a cozy, improbable tale.

How I can be so willfully blind sometimes amazes even me. Well, now I had a story I liked better.

In the course of directing a burglary—an activity which was his avocation—Victor Farkas had come into possession of letters between Tonia Konig and Val Frazier. That was the only coincidence, and *that* was the event which had set all the others in motion. Farkas knew he had hit gold, because he had kept a scrapbook on all the events in the life of Baxter Buchanan, his old Air Force hero, for lo these twenty-five years, including Buchanan's marriage. The information contained in the letters—that Valerie was in thought, if not in deed, being unfaithful to Buchanan—must have pushed Farkas' crazy button. Presumably Buchanan had confided in him sometime during their wartime careers about the first philandering Mrs. Buchanan, and how her infidelity had cut him to the quick. Poor sensitive soul. I was willing to bet that Farkas never forgot that little story. Then, years later, when James Harrington and Mark Jerome presented him with the letters, he had the key. Something that would unlock his hero's gratitude. All he had to do was scare Val back into Buchanan's arms. But of course he couldn't risk harming Val, so he picked on Tonia. What did he expect to get in return from Buchanan? I had no idea. Money? Maybe. Buchanan's undying gratitude? Perhaps. Power over the man? Possibly.

And what about Buchanan? Had he known anything about Farkas' little scheme to bring Val to heel? I guessed not. Farkas probably wanted to present him with a *fait accompli.*

I frowned. This theory had as many holes in it as a hunk of Swiss cheese. Why had Farkas intended to prolong the blackmail process? Did he think he would wear Val down gradually—abrade her by degrees until she went running back to the safety of a socially acceptable relationship? Maybe. And why such gleeful persecution of Tonia? Was that merely an added bonus—the opportunity to harass and humiliate one of the hated female sex? If so, he had certainly thrown himself into his work with inventive abandon.

This whole scheme might have gone along as planned except for one thing. Me. I wondered what had happened earlier tonight. Had Farkas, thinking I knew everything, decided to beat me to Buchanan and confess? It seemed so. And had Buchanan, in a fit of appalled horror at Farkas' activities, his political career at stake, resolved to silence everyone who knew about the half-baked blackmail scheme? And now that he knew about Valerie's infidelity, so to speak, was she about to follow his first wife, and become another victim of his homicidal jealousy?

If so, then poor Buchanan—his night's work was unfinished. There were still two of us running around loose who knew what Farkas had been up to. Lester Baines. And me. And, of course, he still had the problem of Val.

I parked on the street across from the Buchanans' condo apartment, and wondered how I was going to get someone to talk to me. Vacationing on the mainland were they? In a pig's eye. I was willing to bet that Buchanan was haunting the city looking for Lester, and Val was upstairs blissfully oblivious to all these machinations.

Squinting through the fog, I saw the open mouth of the parking garage. Perhaps a tour of the residents' automobiles would tell me if Baxter was in or out. Then I could concentrate on wearing down Val's housekeeper. Or getting her out of bed to answer the phone.

As I had hoped, Buchanan was out. At least the car I had seen at the studio, the one whose vanity plate read WINNER, was gone. Val's white Porsche was there, however.

I ran across the street to the pay phone at the marina, and dialed Val's number again. This time I let it ring. Twenty-nine rings later a sleepy Scottish voice answered. It was the obstructionist housekeeper.

"This is Doctor Reece from Jubilee Hospital," I said in my most officious voice. "I must speak to Ms. Frazier at once."

"I'm sorry—" the housekeeper began.

"Madam," I interrupted. "I must insist. It's about Mr. Buchanan. There's been an accident and we must contact next of kin." Half a lie, but who cared at a time like this?

Silence. Then, amazingly, acquiescence. "Very well. Please hold the line." Vacationing in the Okanagan, eh? Sure.

"Hello?"

I hardly recognized Val's voice. It sounded slurred. Drugged. A shiver ran up my spine. "Val, it's Caitlin. Baxter isn't there, is he?"

"Um . . . no," she said, sounding terrible.

"Where is he?"

"Well . . . I'm not sure. At the office? Or did he go to his farm? I just can't think. Baxter gave me some pills, and I've been sleeping, you see."

"Are you all right?" Ye gods. So he'd drugged her.

"What day is this?" she asked.

"Saturday. No, Sunday now."

"Did you . . . "

"Call off the blackmailer? Yes. But there's a little problem."

"Oh?"

I doubted if shee could stay awake long enough to hear about it, so I didn't bother explaining. There were more important things to impress upon her.

"Valerie, listen to me. You can't stay there. Baxter will be back, and he's likely to do something terrible."

Silence.

"Valerie, answer me!"

"Yes," she mumbled. "I'm here."

"Did you understand what I said?"

"Hmm? What?"

This wasn't going to work. "Get your housekeeper to buzz me up when I ring your apartment from the lobby," I said.

"All right."

To my surprise, when I got there and rang the bell marked Frazier, the door buzzed at once. I leaped for it before someone changed her mind, and ran to the elevators. On the penthouse floor I loped along to P1 and pounded on Val's door. A feisty little woman in a blue quilted dressing gown barred my way. I pushed her aside.

"Val?" I called.

"I'm in here," a slurred voice called from the apartment's nether regions.

She was in her bedroom and, to my surprise, about half dressed. Perhaps what I had told her *had* made some impression after all. She pulled on a pair of fawn wool pants, tucked a dark green shirt into them, and ran her hands over her hair. I picked up her purse from the dresser and held it out to her.

"Caitlin, I have to go to work tomorrow. I need some things."

"Buy them," I told her. "Let's just get out of here."

"All right," she said in a dazed, frightened voice.

I traded glares with the housekeeper, then held my breath, fingers crossed, as the elevator arrived. Mercifully for my jangled nerves, it was empty. It looked as if I might be able to do something right yet.

I waited at the Oak Bay Beach Hotel's registration desk while a sleepy clerk signed in an even more sleepy Val. When I judged she was safely on her way up the stairs to the second floor, I raced back outside to my MG and roared off down the dark, empty streets.

A quick tour revealed that Buchanan wasn't at Lester's new house, or at the house on Redfern Street. I had to conclude that he had given up and gone away. Or gone home. As I was about to do. By now it was close to five in the morning. I thought about the dead people in the house on Redfern, and the living ones in my house on Monterey, and decided to wait to call Sandy. I was in way over my head—it was certainly time for the police. But a few more hours wouldn't matter. The dead didn't need me. Tonia and Lester did.

Chapter 18

Home. I took a fond look at my dark, quiet house, turned off the MG's engine, and hauled myself wearily out of the driver's seat. The steps to the front door seemed especially steep and numerous, and I sighed as I locked the door behind me, tossing my windbreaker over a chair in the living room. I'd just clean up a little before going upstairs, I thought. I washed my face, and deliberately avoided looking at myself in the mirror. Failure is never a pretty sight. Well, maybe Lester and Tonia wouldn't dwell on the subject.

I wondered what to tell Malcolm and Yvonne about their unexpected house guests. Maybe the truth. It would blow my cover as a business consultant, but what the hell. The two of them weren't due home until Sunday about noon—gosh, I had hours and hours to dream something up if I so chose. I turned on my bedside light and kicked off my sneakers. Dizzy with fatigue, I took off my .357, wrapped my leather belt around the holstered gun, and put it on the bookcase. Where was Repo, I wondered. Unless he had somehow gotten upstairs in all the coming and going earlier tonight, he should have been in evidence, sitting eloquently in the middle of my bed, eyeing me with reproachful yellow orbs for keeping such late hours.

"Repo?" I said.

Then the closet door burst open and an enormous piece of the darkness hurled itself at me—a shape with hands that reached for my throat and eyes that burned with cold fire. Fatigue and surprise made me slow, and the shape grabbed me. I cried out in alarm and twisted away, feeling the stitches break loose in my shoulder, falling backwards and hitting the side of my head on a sharp corner of the bed frame. A sunburst exploded behind my eyes, and consciousness began to slip away. I never did see a face, and my last thought was one of abject terror—the Dark Lady had finally found me.

* * * * *

There was a hot throbbing pain in my shoulder, an unbearable pounding in my head, and I wanted to tell whoever was thumping so noisily on the ceiling to stop. But I also wanted to stay in whatever dark, safe place this was. I couldn't remember why I shouldn't open my eyes, so I did. A mistake. I was lying on my bedroom floor where I had fallen, my body twisted to one side, my nose on the floorboards in a puddle of blood. What had happened? Alarmed, I turned my head, and someone prodded me with a foot. Then I remembered, and opened my eyes. On the floor about four feet away from me crouched Baxter Buchanan. How had he found me? Val. Of course. He'd extracted enough information from the drugged Val . . .

200

"Awake, I see," he said. "Good. We can do this one of two ways: the hard way or the easy way. It's up to you."

I struggled to sit up. "Do what?" I managed. "Why should I cooperate with you? You're going to kill me anyhow."

He laughed. "How very perceptive of you, my dear."

I looked at the gun in his hand. It was a US officer's model Colt .45 automatic. It would make a horrible noise, but I guessed Buchanan intended to be well away before the neighbors came to investigate. I decided this was no time to take affront at his patronizing remarks. I should address myself instead to the problem of how to get at my own gun which was directly behind Buchanan on the bookcase. I leaned back against my nightstand, and touched my head gingerly. I had an egg-sized lump on my temple, and it was sticky with blood. It hurt like hell, and worse, it had affected my vision. I couldn't focus properly. If I looked directly at Buchanan, there were at least three of him. I closed my eyes, feeling nauseated. Not now, I told myself. You can be sick later.

"It won't work, Buchanan," I told him. I needed to engage him in conversation. Stall.

"Oh? what won't work?"

I made a global gesture with the arm not immobilized by pain. "What you've done. It's too late to keep it quiet."

"Ah, but that's why I'm here," he said. "Of course it's not too late. That's what we're going to chat about." So that's why he hadn't yet finished me off—he needed to know who I'd been talking to. Good. If he thought I had something he needed, he would have to give me the thing I needed most—time.

I tried a laugh. It sounded a trifle panicked to me, and I hoped he hadn't noticed. "Forget it, Buchanan. Even if I told you what you want to know, it won't do you any good."

"What do you mean?" he asked, a note of doubt creeping into his voice.

"The trail for this night's work will lead right back to you." I embellished a little more. "No, it's too late to cover up."

He stood up, and took a few steps away from me. "You're wrong there," he told me. "Mistakes can always be covered up."

"Come off it, Buchanan. You can't kill us all and expect to walk away from this."

"Why not?" he said, smiling. "That fool Farkas was doing the blackmailing, not me. He and his young friends had a falling out. The disagreement led to murder." He shrugged. "There's no way to connect any of this to me."

"Farkas really messed things up for you, didn't he?" I taunted, trying to distract him. "If he'd just left well enough alone, none of this needed to happen."

Buchanan smiled. "True. But he paid for his meddling. I don't need anyone's help to chastise my own wife."

Chastise? Was that what he thought he was doing thirty-one years ago? "Are you going to chastise Val?"

He gave me a flat, unblinking reptilian stare, and I shivered. "Oh yes," he said. "She'll pay."

This was crazy. He didn't really think he could do these things and get away with them, did he?

"What a lot of problems Victor Farkas caused for you," I tried again. Damn it, there had to be a way to provoke him. "And to think he was only trying to help you. That's a rotten way to repay someone's devotion, Buchanan. Or was it more than devotion? How close did you two get overseas, anyhow?"

He stared at me, the gun steady in his fist.

I decided to try something else. "Val wasn't cheating on you, Baxter," I told him. I saw a flicker of interest in his eyes and forged ahead. Hell, maybe I could appeal to his conscience. "Farkas was an idiot. If he had read the letters more carefully he'd have known that Val never did anything with Tonia. But once he realized he had an entrée to your gratitude, he couldn't think of anything else. There was no need for any elaborate plot to get her to go back to you." I decided not to tell him that Val had intended to leave him anyhow. Better to concentrate on the positive aspects, like Val's innocence. "You didn't have to kill Farkas and the boys. Just like you don't have to kill me. Or anyone else."

"Oh, I do," he said sorrowfully. "You don't seem to understand. My political future is at stake here, too. No one must ever know any of this."

It wasn't going to work. Buchanan had his mind made up. Well, maybe I *should* mention Val's plans for leaving him. What did I have to lose? If I could make him angry, distract him long enough, I could make a lunge, grab my own gun, and equalize the odds a little. I wondered how implacable he'd be staring down the barrel of my .357.

"You're a crazy man," I told him heatedly. "Do you know that? You murdered your first wife, you've killed three people tonight, and you're standing here talking about killing three more. When did you finally lose it, Buchanan? When you murdered the first woman you imagined was philandering?" I forced a laugh. "I don't blame her a bit. Or Val. No one should have to live with a psychopath."

That did it. His florid face turned dark red, and he took one step toward me. As he drew back his foot to deliver a kick, I realized that my desire to provoke him had backfired. His foot landed squarely in my ribs, and I expelled a whuff of air. I barely had time to roll into a ball as he kicked me again, and this time I heard a rib crack. No good, Caitlin, no good.

"So we'll do this the hard way," he said, panting a little from such unaccustomed exertion. "It doesn't matter. Oh, you'll talk to me, all right. And after I've finished you off, I'll attend to the others. You don't understand, do you? I *will* get away with this."

Atta boy, Baxter. Kill us all. I had to do something fast, because soon I'd be unable to do anything. He'd simply kick me into insensibility and shoot me. Taking one pain-racked breath, I got my feet underneath me, and lurched off the floor at him. It would have worked, but I miscalculated how disoriented and weak I was. I tottered, grabbed for his gun hand, and he slapped me down. It was all over. I couldn't summon the strength to get up again. I rolled over so I could see him. If he was going to sheet me, he'd damn well have to look me in the eye. He raised the gun and aimed it at my head. The opening in the end of the muzzle seemed as big and black as a mine shaft. There was nothing to do but wait for the bullet.

I heard the floorboards creak and at the same time saw the white flash of her arms. Buchanan heard something too, because he started to turn his head in the direction of the sound. But Tonia was already completing her swing. My heavy Smith Corona portable typewriter descended on Buchanan's head with a thunk like an axe hitting wood. His eyes rolled back in his head, and he fell towards the bed, discharging his gun as he did so. The bullet missed my head by six inches, and I felt it fan my face as it went by. Then Buchanan slid off the bed and lay on the floor beside me, one hand outstretched as if in supplication. His baffled brown eyes were wide open, and very dead. I looked up at Tonia.

She stood in the bedroom doorway, pale as a ghost. Looking at her hands as if they, not she, had done this horrible thing, she wiped them on the sides of her jeans. "We heard noises," she said. "I came down to see what was happening. When I saw him about to kill you, I . . . I . . . I had to do something." She looked at me for confirmation. "I had to do it, Caitlin."

"Yes," I told her. "You did." Not quite the truth, but close.

"But my God, I've killed him."

"You saved my life," I said, shifting the focus a little.

She looked from Buchanan to me, and blinked several times. "Yes, I did, didn't I?" she said. She nodded as if the idea made sense to her.

I hoped it did, because when she had the leisure to reflect on this, she was going to realize that she had traded her philosophy for a human life. Mine. Caitlin Reece, thug. Had it been a fair trade? I was the wrong person to ask. Only Tonia could answer that question.

Chapter 19

I lay on the couch in a pleasant haze of inebriation. Bach's Cantata 147, *Jesu, Joy of Man's Desiring,* was playing, and I was struck again by the chill beauty of that wonderfully *mathematical* music. There's nothing like Bach to convince you that God's in her heaven and all's right with the world. Of course, a little Glenfiddich Scotch—a gift from a very grateful client—was proving helpful, too. I poured myself another dram. Toasting Repo, who lay beside me playing nursemaid, I thought with a surge of glee that I had absolutely nothing to do this afternoon. Nowhere I was supposed to be. No one to see. Nobody's problems that required attention. I could just lie here and vegetate.

Nor did I want to think much about the activities of today's earlier hours. They bore too much resemblance to the last act of *Hamlet*. I was genuinely grieved that Lester's friends had had to die. I couldn't say the same about Victor Farkas. Or Baxter Buchanan. Well, at least Val was finally free of him.

The window was open behind me, and happy chirping sounds floated in from the garden. The robins had resumed nest building now that the sun had come out. I stretched luxuriously. Life might be worth living after all.

On the coffee table was an enormous bunch of daffodils and tulips from Gray. Good grief, you'd think I was convalescing or something. Just to prove I wasn't a complete invalid, I sat up. Not too bad. My rib protested only a little, my shoulder itched just a bit, and my newly sutured head throbbed, but it was nothing incapacitating. It had better not be. I had business to do next week: lunch with Virginia; long overdue trip to Texada Island to see Jan; dinner with Sandy and Mary; and the pursuit of Yvonne and Malcolm's slippery Oliver Renbo, he of the Rainbow Fund. But that was next week. This was now.

The strains of the cantata came to an end, and I sighed. I'm not exactly a believer in God, but from time to time I find it comforting to think that there might be a guiding hand in all this mess. A pattern. A meaning. I looked over my shoulder at the robins in the apple tree and smiled.

Reaching past Repo, I turned off the stereo. He protested, and I apologized. One should never antagonize one's nurse.

"You'll like this," I told him, turning on the television. "It'll be educational. More fun than Big Bird."

"Mraff," he opined skeptically.

"Oh, give it a chance. Look," I told him, "there's someone you know. Your favorite bedmate. Next to me, that is."

He perked up, seeming to recognize the voice.

It was the end of the televised debate at U Vic on nonviolent alternatives to war. I hadn't been very interested in hearing what the debaters had to say, thug that I am, but I did want to check in on Tonia. With relief I saw that she seemed to be suffering no ill effects from her early morning ordeal. That would come later, I supposed—she'd had a big blow to her principles. For the time being, however, she seemed to be functioning fairly well.

She looked good, I was pleased to see. Her glossy black hair shone, and she was wearing a vivid blue sweater that made her eyes look like pieces of lapis lazuli. She had a terrific television presence, and when she looked straight into the camera lens, you were sure she was talking directly to you. After I had missed half of what she was saying, I realized she *was* talking to me.

" . . . happened to me recently," she told me. "A crisis of faith. I, and my beliefs, were put to the test. I like to think that I made the right choice." She smiled a little ruefully. "I will now have to amend my long held assertion that violence is never a viable option in conflict resolution. Because of course, it is." Then she turned to the audience to answer a question. I switched off the television.

"So, the estimable Dr. Konig is battered but unbowed," I commented to Repo.

He didn't answer, which was just as well. I couldn't have replied. There was suddenly another lump in my throat, and my lower lip started to quiver. I even felt, or fancied I felt, a pang in that region of the romantic anatomy commonly called the heart. It's just the weather, you fool, I chastised myself through an attack of watering eyes. Probably a cloud of errant pollen from the apple tree. Everyone knows spring can be a tricky season. I blew my nose several times, dried my eyes, and lay back down on the couch. More Bach, I decided. And more Glenfiddich. And get a grip on yourself, Reece. You can't lie here sniveling like someone's maiden aunt—it's bad for client morale. What if someone were to phone? To hell with it, I thought uncharitably, I need *my* rest, too.

I closed my eyes, willing the telephone silent, the fearful brave, the needy self sufficient, the cat quiescent, and the doorbell mute. For a few hours, anyhow.

It worked.

A few of the publications of
THE NAIAD PRESS, INC.
P.O. Box 10543 • Tallahassee, Florida 32302
Phone (904) 539-9322
Mail orders welcome. Please include 15% postage.

MEMORY BOARD by Jane Rule. 336 pp. Memorable novel about an aging lesbian couple.　　ISBN 0-941483-02-9　　$8.95

THE ALWAYS ANONYMOUS BEAST by Lauren Wright Douglas. 224 pp. A Caitlin Reece mystery. First in a series.
ISBN 0-941483-04-5　　8.95

SEARCHING FOR SPRING by Patricia A. Murphy. 224 pp. Novel about the recovery of love.　　ISBN 0-941483-00-2　　8.95

DUSTY'S QUEEN OF HEARTS DINER by Lee Lynch. 240 pp. Romantic blue-collar novel.　　ISBN 0-941483-01-0　　8.95

PARENTS MATTER by Ann Muller. 240 pp. Parents' relationships with lesbian daughters and gay sons.
ISBN 0-930044-91-6　　9.95

THE PEARLS by Shelley Smith. 176 pp. Passion and fun in the Caribbean sun.　　ISBN 0-930044-93-2　　7.95

MAGDALENA by Sarah Aldridge. 352 pp. Epic Lesbian novel set on three continents.　　ISBN 0-930044-99-1　　8.95

THE BLACK AND WHITE OF IT by Ann Allen Shockley. 144 pp. Short stories.　　ISBN 0-930044-96-7　　$7.95

SAY JESUS AND COME TO ME by Ann Allen Shockley. 288 pp. Contemporary romance.　　ISBN 0-930044-98-3　　8.95

LOVING HER by Ann Allen Shockley. 192 pp. Romantic love story.　　ISBN 0-930044-97-5　　7.95

MURDER AT THE NIGHTWOOD BAR by Katherine V. Forrest. 240 pp. A Kate Delafield mystery. Second in a series.
ISBN 0-930044-92-4　　8.95

ZOE'S BOOK by Gail Pass. 224 pp. Passionate, obsessive love story.　　ISBN 0-930044-95-9　　7.95

WINGED DANCER by Camarin Grae. 228 pp. Erotic Lesbian adventure story.　　ISBN 0-930044-88-6　　8.95

PAZ by Camarin Grae. 336 pp. Romantic Lesbian adventurer with the power to change the world.　　ISBN 0-930044-89-4　　8.95

SOUL SNATCHER by Camarin Grae. 224 pp. A puzzle, an adventure, a mystery—Lesbian romance.
ISBN 0-930044-90-8　　8.95

THE LOVE OF GOOD WOMEN by Isabel Miller. 224 pp. Long-awaited new novel by the author of the beloved *Patience and Sarah*.　　ISBN 0-930044-81-9　　8.95

THE HOUSE AT PELHAM FALLS by Brenda Weathers. 240 pp. Suspenseful Lesbian ghost story.　　ISBN 0-930044-79-7　　7.95

THE BURNTON WIDOWS by Vicki P. McConnell. 272 pp. A
Nyla Wade mystery, second in the series. ISBN 0-930044-52-5   7.95

OLD DYKE TALES by Lee Lynch. 224 pp. Extraordinary
stories of our diverse Lesbian lives.   ISBN 0-930044-51-7   7.95

DAUGHTERS OF A CORAL DAWN by Katherine V. Forrest.
240 pp. Novel set in a Lesbian new world. ISBN 0-930044-50-9   7.95

THE PRICE OF SALT by Claire Morgan. 288 pp. A milestone
novel, a beloved classic.   ISBN 0-930044-49-5   8.95

AGAINST THE SEASON by Jane Rule. 224 pp. Luminous,
complex novel of interrelationships.   ISBN 0-930044-48-7   7.95

LOVERS IN THE PRESENT AFTERNOON by Kathleen
Fleming. 288 pp. A novel about recovery and growth.
                                          ISBN 0-930044-46-0   8.95

TOOTHPICK HOUSE by Lee Lynch. 264 pp. Love between
two Lesbians of different classes.   ISBN 0-930044-45-2   7.95

MADAME AURORA by Sarah Aldridge. 256 pp. Historical
novel featuring a charismatic "seer."   ISBN 0-930044-44-4   7.95

CURIOUS WINE by Katherine V. Forrest. 176 pp. Passionate
Lesbian love story, a best-seller.   ISBN 0-930044-43-6   7.95

BLACK LESBIAN IN WHITE AMERICA by Anita Cornwell.
141 pp. Stories, essays, autobiography.   ISBN 0-930044-41-X   7.50

CONTRACT WITH THE WORLD by Jane Rule. 340 pp.
Powerful, panoramic novel of gay life.   ISBN 0-930044-28-2   7.95

YANTRAS OF WOMANLOVE by Tee A. Corinne. 64 pp.
Photos by noted Lesbian photographer.   ISBN 0-930044-30-4   6.95

MRS. PORTER'S LETTER by Vicki P. McConnell. 224 pp.
The first Nyla Wade mystery.   ISBN 0-930044-29-0   7.95

TO THE CLEVELAND STATION by Carol Anne Douglas.
192 pp. Interracial Lesbian love story.   ISBN 0-930044-27-4   6.95

THE NESTING PLACE by Sarah Aldridge. 224 pp. A
three-woman triangle—love conquers all! ISBN 0-930044-26-6   7.95

THIS IS NOT FOR YOU by Jane Rule. 284 pp. A letter to a
beloved is also an intricate novel.   ISBN 0-930044-25-8   7.95

FAULTLINE by Sheila Ortiz Taylor. 140 pp. Warm, funny,
literate story of a startling family.   ISBN 0-930044-24-X   6.95

THE LESBIAN IN LITERATURE by Barbara Grier. 3d ed.
Foreword by Maida Tilchen. 240 pp. Comprehensive bibliography. Literary ratings; rare photos.   ISBN 0-930044-23-1   7.95

ANNA'S COUNTRY by Elizabeth Lang. 208 pp. A woman
finds her Lesbian identity.   ISBN 0-930044-19-3   6.95

PRISM by Valerie Taylor. 158 pp. A love affair between two
women in their sixties.   ISBN 0-930044-18-5   6.95

BLACK LESBIANS: AN ANNOTATED BIBLIOGRAPHY
compiled by J.R. Roberts. Foreword by Barbara Smith. 112
pp. Award winning bibliography.   ISBN 0-930044-21-5   5.95

THE MARQUISE AND THE NOVICE by Victoria Ramstetter. 108 pp. A Lesbian Gothic novel. ISBN 0-930044-16-9   4.95

OUTLANDER by Jane Rule. 207 pp. Short stories and essays by one of our finest writers. ISBN 0-930044-17-7   6.95

SAPPHISTRY: THE BOOK OF LESBIAN SEXUALITY by Pat Califia. 2d edition, revised. 195 pp. ISBN 0-930044-47-9   7.95

ALL TRUE LOVERS by Sarah Aldridge. 292 pp. Romantic novel set in the 1930s and 1940s. ISBN 0-930044-10-X   7.95

A WOMAN APPEARED TO ME by Renee Vivien. 65 pp. A classic; translated by Jeannette H. Foster. ISBN 0-930044-06-1   5.00

CYTHEREA'S BREATH by Sarah Aldridge. 240 pp. Romantic novel about women's entrance into medicine. 0-930044-02-9   6.95

TOTTIE by Sarah Aldridge. 181 pp. Lesbian romance in the turmoil of the sixties. ISBN 0-930044-01-0   6.95

THE LATECOMER by Sarah Aldridge. 107 pp. A delicate love story. ISBN 0-930044-00-2   5.00

ODD GIRL OUT by Ann Bannon   ISBN 0-930044-83-5   5.95
I AM A WOMAN by Ann Bannon.   ISBN 0-930044-84-3   5.95
WOMEN IN THE SHADOWS by Ann Bannon.
    ISBN 0-930044-85-1   5.95
JOURNEY TO A WOMAN by Ann Bannon.
    ISBN 0-930044-86-X   5.95
BEEBO BRINKER by Ann Bannon   ISBN 0-930044-87-8   5.95

Legendary novels written in the fifties and sixties, set in the gay mecca of Greenwich Village.

VOLUTE BOOKS

JOURNEY TO FULFILLMENT   Early classics by Valerie   3.95
A WORLD WITHOUT MEN   Taylor: The Erika Frohmann   3.95
RETURN TO LESBOS   series.   3.95

These are just a few of the many Naiad Press titles—we are the oldest and largest lesbian/feminist publishing company in the world. Please request a complete catalog. We offer personal service; we encourage and welcome direct mail orders from individuals who have limited access to bookstores carrying our publications.